"I'm hit!" Lyo

The Ironman stag... clawed to his hands and knees, crawling for cover.

Then something hit the floor with a thump. Lyons instinctively knew what it was before he even saw it.

A grenade!

Suddenly a searing ball of white light exploded into the room. The concussion slammed into him.

As the shock waves diminished he became aware of movement. He made out a stocky shape in the drifting smoke.

"Pol...over here." The words were nothing more than a hoarse whisper, but the figure heard it and began to move toward Lyons. With a jolt, Lyons realized the stocky figure was not Blancanales.

It was Kadal. The assassin. Slowly he raised his right arm and pointed at Lyons's prone form.

It was then that Lyons saw the gun in his hand.

Mack Bolan's

ABLE TEAM

ABLE TEAM

HARD KILL

Dick Stivers

A GOLD EAGLE BOOK FROM

WORLDWIDE

TORONTO · NEW YORK · LONDON · PARIS
AMSTERDAM · STOCKHOLM · HAMBURG
ATHENS · MILAN · TOKYO · SYDNEY

First edition August 1986

ISBN 0-373-61225-7

Special thanks and acknowledgment to
Chuck Rogers for his contributions to this work.

Printed in Canada

PROLOGUE

The room was all black—black walls, black floors, black ceiling. Even the poker table was covered in black felt instead of green.

Carl Lyons sat on one side of the table. On the other sat Death, a skeleton draped in a coarse black shroud.

When the game started, there had been other players. But now they were all gone. They had lost or folded, then had vanished into the claustrophobic gloom of the room. It was down to the Ironman and the Deadman, the Grim Reaper himself.

The game was blackjack, twenty-one. Death was dealing. Lyons checked his hand.

A queen and a nine. Nineteen. A good hand. Not great, but good. Nearly damned good. Anytime the odds were good going on damned good, you were lucky, he thought. Especially in this business.

"I'll stand," the Ironman said, leaning back in his chair.

Lyons glimpsed the skull's perpetual grin beneath the shroud. The eye sockets were vacant, black voids boring into Lyons's brain. "This time, I will win," the skeleton said. "You are mine."

"Someday, maybe," Lyons agreed. "In fact, someday for sure. But not for a long time, asshole."

"Now," replied the skeleton. "Not someday, but now."

The skeleton turned over his cards. A nine and a four. Thirteen. He gave himself a hit.

Make it a face card, Lyons thought. Or a ten. Bust the bastard.

The card turned over. A three. Sixteen. The shrouded figure uttered an eerie laugh, devoid of mirth, a hollow sound from the grave.

Damn. Lyons did some mental arithmetic. Six will bust him. Make it a six or better.

Another hit. The card slid off the top of the deck. A deuce. Eighteen. Lyons looked up at the bony visage, mesmerized. The room felt hot, and the walls seemed to close in on him.

The skeleton leaned forward, leering at Lyons. "Now, Ironman!" he repeated gleefully. "Not later, but now!"

Again, a hit.

An ace. They were tied at nineteen apiece.

The skeleton leaned back, and white teeth parted as a different sound emanated from the skull's mouth, a ghostly cackle that echoed from the bowels of hell itself.

"Another hit!" Death shrieked. "I'll take another hit!"

An ace or a deuce would do it, Lyons realized. And there were still three of each in the deck. Six ways to lose. Six ways to die.

Beads of sweat broke out on his face.

The peals of laughter rang on. The skeleton's arm slid out from the coarse shroud, toward the deck. Slowly the skeletal finger slid the top card off the pack and onto the table. Equally slowly, the thumb and forefinger bracketed the card to flip it over.

The Ironman's hand shot out and pinned the bony wrist to the table, on top of the card.

"To hell with you!" he snarled. "To hell with your rules! I don't care if it's my time or not! I'm not going unless you're tough enough to take me!"

The shrieks of laughter intensified, reverberating off the walls and back into the Ironman's head, mocking him.

"You hear me?" Lyons roared.

The skull looked at him. "I *am* tough enough. Besides, you might like it."

Somehow the bony hand cupping the card slid out from under Lyons's grip.

The Ironman tensed. He felt himself losing control, slipping, as the two clawlike hands started to move toward his face, his throat . . .

With a shout, Lyons sat bolt upright, soaked in sweat. He remained there for a long time, sitting still in the darkness, wondering what that last card was, and wondering if he could fight it even if he lost.

He didn't fear Death. He just didn't want to lose life.

Losing life would be bad, because living and laughing and feeling things were good, and Death, like a diamond, was forever.

But the dream made him realize something else, too.

He would never surrender to Death. Never give up. Never. It didn't matter what that last card was, Lyons wouldn't pay up willingly. As long as there was life in his body, he would resist the call of the figure in the black robe.

Maybe Death would be tough enough to take him, all right. And maybe it wouldn't.

Still, it was a hell of a frame of mind for the start of a mission.

1

"Tomorrow is my day."

Nobody heard him. There was nobody else in the room. But that didn't stop him from talking, anyway.

He always talked to himself, out loud, when he built the bombs.

Abdel Makhi lived to serve his god. Soon, he hoped to die in that service, here in Beirut, Lebanon. It would be tomorrow—Monday—in fact. The world would not forget him.

It was the way of Hizbullah, the Party of God.

Makhi was a Shiite Muslim by birth and by faith. Beirut was his home. He was born there, and he knew he would soon die there.

The most radical faction of the Muslims, the Shiites were on the move. Like most Muslims, Makhi and other young Shiite men dreamed of liberating Lebanon, of virtually ridding it of anybody who wasn't a Muslim. But while other, more moderate Muslims set about achieving that end by working through government and business, the Shiites had a different idea.

War. Death to the enemies of Islam.

The Shiites were, after all, direct descendants of the original assassins, the *hashshashin*, or hashish eaters, who had come down from their mountain strongholds to murder their political rivals.

Terrorism and martyrdom were better than diplomacy and voting any day.

Abdel Makhi had studied the legends of Hassan Ben Sabbah, the Persian leader who developed the concept of assassination in the eleventh century. With certain convenient modifications, Abdel had adopted that approach for himself.

Ben Sabbah's method had been a practical implementation of the Muslim belief that death in the service of Allah was a glorious thing, to be rewarded by rebirth in paradise. To give his followers a glimpse of what that involved, Ben Sabbah drugged his killers and placed them in a garden. When they awoke from the drugs—legend said it was hashish, or concentrated cannabis—they found themselves enjoying a slice of paradise.

Women. Food. The spectrum of sensual pleasures.

A few days later, again drugged into insensibility, the killers would be returned to their own residences. The effect of it all was as of a dream, a vision of the paradise that awaited them if they died while killing for Allah.

Abdel's approach involved some of the same aspects, but he had to supply his own earthly delights beforehand.

In some respects, however, Abdel was a loser.

The preceding evening, he had attended to the secular side of things by first engaging a prostitute and then scoring a gram of coke, a slug of hash and some other white powder represented to be methamphetamine. His personal glimpse of the paradise promised by Ben Sabbah had been slightly marred, however, when the chemicals had adversely affected his ability to fully partake of the carnal aspects of his plan.

But the experience had done nothing to lessen his ardor as far as his planned mass homicide was concerned.

"Tomorrow is my day," Abdel said aloud again. "Things will be better in paradise, and I shall have left the world better off than before."

He turned back to the task at hand—four hundred pounds of high explosive carefully packed into the back of an old panel truck. Three detonating mechanisms, all separate, so there was no way the massive bomb could fail to go off. And because Abdel believed that the simple details are often the ones that go wrong, as a final fall-back, he would carry a conventional hand grenade.

Abdel Makhi smiled in satisfaction. There was no chance of failure.

"I will be alive," he said. "I will be alive until I go to martyrdom and the glory of Islam."

To see that he stayed alive, Abdel Makhi had modified the old truck in several ways.

Though he didn't expect any heavily armed guards when he made his drive-up approach—the American fools evidently thought the facility was both secret and harmless, so security was relatively minimal—Abdel had nonetheless taken some basic precautions to make the van harder to disable.

He had bolted metal plates across the front and to each side of the old four-cylinder engine. He wouldn't be driving it far enough to have any problem with overheating.

He replaced the pneumatic tires with solid rubber ones.

He attached still other armor around the driver's seat, including a heavy slab of steel across the windshield, with holes drilled to see through.

"I am the assassin," he said aloud. "I kill for my God, and for Hizbullah."

Hizbullah was a faction within the Shiites. Just as the Shiites were the most radical of the Muslims, Hizbullah was the most radical of the Shiites.

Abdel Makhi had dreamed of the day that he knew tomorrow would be. A day of glory for Islam, for Lebanon, for the Shiites, for Hizbullah.

For himself.

A day of death for the American imperialist oppressors who operated out of what looked like another ordinary building in Beirut.

Abdel knew all about it. Building 101, as the Americans called it, was used by the CIA as a headquarters for secret missions in Lebanon. It housed translators, readers and watchers, bureaucrats who collected information to be used against the Muslims.

He knew because he had seen it himself.

The anonymous-looking building had been mentioned by one of the other members of Hizbullah. The man was a friend of Abdel's, and had a sister who learned about Building 101 a month or so previously from a junior member of the American diplomatic corps.

The budding statesman had told her over drinks one night. He had been trying to impress the pretty, dark—and, by the standards of the Middle East, liberated—young woman. To that end, he had made the building and its activities sound more clandestine than it really was. It really didn't matter, he thought; it was only a minor breach of security, and besides, the building was due to be vacated in a few weeks, anyway.

In fact, Building 101 was one of those older, nondescript buildings leased by the American government and used on a short-term basis for whatever was needed.

For the past eight months, that need had been to provide temporary quarters for a corps of translators. And, yes, the translators did work for the CIA—indirectly, anyway. But their job had no secret-agent duties. Instead, they had the generally boring job of translating local newspapers, handbills and periodicals, simply to learn what was being reported in the media.

No "sources," which was the jargon for informants. No "deep throat" insiders passing out information. No secret drop-box locations, no assas-

sination tools disguised as ballpoint pens. Just a bunch
of bureaucrats and graduate students translating what
the press put out.

Abdel didn't know all this, of course.

He should have guessed it from the almost total lack
of security at the place. Apart from the last guy out
locking up at night, there wasn't any. He also could
have learned that, starting with the lobby reception-
ist, most of the people who worked in 101 were listed
in the phone book. His hatred and contempt for the
Americans, however, blinded him to such details.

Maybe it wouldn't have made any difference if he
had known it.

"There is no glory but Islam!" he shouted to the
empty room.

At age twenty-seven, Makhi had seen Lebanon
ground down by the PLO, the Palestine Liberation
Organization. Then came the Israelis—in 1982, they
"liberated" Lebanon—and a new era of freedom was
foreseen for Lebanon and the Muslims.

That vision proved to be short-lived. Within two
years, the Shiites had taken up arms against the Israelis, and the blood continued to flow into the desert
sand.

The Shiites had compiled an impressive resume of
terror and revenge, largely directed against anybody
Western and bigger than they were.

By 1985, they controlled West Beirut. Other Shiites
had driven other trucks loaded with explosives against

the U.S. Marines, and had played a major role in the hijacking of Flight 847.

Abdel shared a dream of his fellow Hizbullah followers. In his diary, he wrote, "Someday I will die in a suicide mission against the enemies of Islam. I pray it will be the United States."

"Tomorrow," he snarled. Then his features softened, and he repeated it, almost lovingly. "Tomorrow is my day."

DALE MARTIN RAN A WEARY HAND through his graying hair as he spoke into the telephone. "Dammit, Frank, don't you have any other place to put 'em besides here?"

The voice on the other end of the line crackled a reply. "You guys are out of the place, aren't you?"

"Out? Hell, yes, we're out. Lock, stock and barrel," Dale replied.

"And it's got new carpeting, right?"

"Well, yeah, sure. But the place is so damned plain. No place for a bunch of school kids, for God's sake."

"Don't sweat that. These are good kids. We'll get some cots from the Red Cross. Make it a big adventure. It's only for one night, anyway."

A career bureaucrat, Dale had been with the State Department for nearly twenty years. He held a mid-level administrative post in the Translations Bureau, or T.B., as it was known. He was a kindly man with kids in college, who had risen to where he was by working hard and being a nice guy. He lacked the killer instinct to rise any higher, and was content with himself and his spot.

Shaking his head, Dale thought it over. The past two weeks had been tough.

First, Administration had decided to lay new carpeting in Building 101. The carpeting had been budgeted and on the agenda for six months; finally, two weeks before T.B. was supposed to vacate, they got around to laying it.

"Look, why not wait two weeks? Then we'll be out of there, and the carpet layers can take their time, and not have to work around anybody."

"Sorry," said the man from Administration. "It's got to be now."

So they had called in a bunch of workmen, who had ripped up the old carpet and installed the new one while the employees assigned to the T.B. had packed up for the move. Then the move itself had turned into a nightmare.

It wasn't scheduled until the next week. But Admin had decided the only time good for the movers was last week. So the overtime had been approved, the packing completed at night. Finally, by Friday, the job was done. No trace of T.B. remained in Building 101.

The events of the past two weeks had made Dale hope he never saw Building 101 again.

And now this, thought Dale wearily. He was technically still in charge of the facility, so when Frank Dennison wanted to use it to warehouse his cultural exchange group of thirty kids for a day and a night, Dale was the man to see.

Stalling, Dale asked for the second time, "How old are they?"

"I told you. Ages seven to nine. Members of the International Culture Club. Rich parents, but you can't hold that against the kids. They're a pretty good bunch, considering. Besides, it's only for one night, until Admin straightens out the screw-up at the Embassy."

Dale sighed in resignation. "Okay. When do you need to get in?"

"First thing in the morning. Start getting things set up. The kids will be through with the day's activities about one, so they'll be there after that."

"You're on."

Dale met Frank Dennison at the building shortly after seven on Monday. Dale stayed and helped Frank get things ready to bivouac the kids.

When the children finally arrived, he was glad he had stayed to help.

Frank was right. They were a good bunch of kids. They "fell to" enthusiastically.

One of the older boys, a towheaded lad of nine, had attended a year of military academy. He had nominated himself the "squad leader" for the "barracks," and the others elected him.

They promptly moved all the cots from the two back rooms where Frank and Dale had set them up into the big entryway to Building 101. Then they raced around excitedly, choosing their personal spots. The squad leader set about getting the "barracks" in order.

First, he showed them how to make their beds "Army-style." Then he instructed them to stow their gear at the foot of the cots. Also "Army-style."

Finally, he had them all fall out for "barracks inspection" by the commandant, each at the foot of his or her cot. Thirty-one boys and girls—seven, eight, and nine years old—stood at attention while "General" Frank Dennison and his adjutant, "Major" Dale Martin, strode slowly from bed to bed, from one child-stern face to the next.

The two men put on faces of mock severity befitting the solemnity of the occasion. They straightened clothing with little tugs here and there. For some of the older boys, Major Martin put his face inches from theirs, trying to provoke a crack in the stern faces.

The inspection was nearly completed when Abdel Makhi drove his fortified truck through the unlocked front doors of Building 101 to the glory of himself and Hizbullah.

And the detonator worked the first time.

2

"It's too damned dangerous, that's why."

John Harper's voice was flat, definitive. His jaw jutted as he spoke.

Nobody responded. A tight silence descended over the conference room. One minute passed, then another. They were marked off by the long second hand that swept around the face of a clock high on the wall above the head of the table.

An ancient ceiling fan hummed energetically above the group. The blades stirred the musty air into sharp movement in the confined room of the building in Los Angeles.

Of the five men present, Harper alone was sitting up close to the table. The only CIA man in the group, he was leaning forward, forearms on the tabletop, urging his point on the others.

The others were Jim Myers and Julie Harris, plus two men from Washington, D.C. Myers and Harris were agents from the FBI's Counterterrorist Squad. The other two had ambiguous titles like Special Assistant to somebody or another in the Justice Department.

Now, as Harper spoke, all except Julie leaned back from the table, legs crossed with one ankle on the other knee. Their arms were either folded over their chests or with fingers laced behind their heads.

Their postures indicated that the message was clear. They didn't want to hear what Harper wanted to say.

Finally FBI agent Jim Myers spoke. He was in his forties, with the makings of a midlife roll around his waist. Unlike the others at the table, he wore a beard. Ostensibly it was part of his cover, but everybody knew that since Myers was a supervisor rather than a field agent, he didn't need cover. The beard actually meant that he was in such good graces with his superiors at the Bureau that he could get away with it.

"Explain that."

Myers had the habit of tucking his chin toward his chest when he spoke, affecting a spurious importance he would never achieve on his own merit.

Harper looked at him with barely concealed disgust.

He despised Myers almost as much as he did the man's beard. The latter he regarded as so unimaginative that it might have been provided by the Bureau, along with one Smith & Wesson Model 10 heavy-barrel .38 and one set of Peerless handcuffs.

The standard FBI-issue beard, he thought sourly.

"What's to explain?" he snapped. "Fadi Kadal is the most dangerous assassin on earth. He never misses. He hits, and then he vanishes for months or years at a time. Every Western country in the world would like to get even a hint as to where he is, and here we are watching him and sitting on our hands.''

"So?" Myers's voice was cold and pompous. "Make your point, man."

"So let's take him out right now. While we can. It's crazy to just hold back and wait for him to go first."

"Why's that?"

"Why's that?" Harper echoed incredulously. "Hell, if he goes underground and we lose him, we'll never find him again."

Myers rolled his eyes ceilingward at this latest cross he had to bear. The operation was delicate enough without having to nursemaid some psycho CIA agent like Harper.

Goddamned Neanderthals didn't understand modern procedures and laws.

"Look," the Bureau agent said, making a show of controlling his temper, "this is a sensitive operation, with orders approved at the highest levels. The *highest* levels, if you get my drift."

"Orders can be changed," Harper retorted. "At the highest levels."

Myers shook his head. "We're not just after Kadal's body. Hell, our source of information is so tight with him we can have that whenever we want it."

"So what are we after that is worth risking losing him?"

"You know the answer to that, Harper. Washington wants to wait until we have enough evidence to prosecute him and convict him, not just rub him out."

"We've got evidence," Harper said.

"We want more. Maybe even wait until he's in the act, so to speak. Then when we take him out, not only do we protect the targets, but the world gets a demonstration that Uncle Sam can handle these terrorists in a civilized yet effective manner."

"Save it for the Kiwanis," muttered Harper.

Myers ignored the barb. "We want other terrorist groups to see that we are not just paying lip service to justice, afraid to step on any toes. We want that as much as we want Kadal himself."

Bullshit, thought the CIA man. It's the publicity you're after. Glory be to you and the Bureau. Well, you're the man in charge, but I'm going on record with my objections, anyway.

"Then we're making a big mistake."

Harper was a rangy, powerful man with close-cropped brown hair and a mustache to match. His appearance conveyed something of the great white hunter toughness.

And, unlike the Bureau agent, Harper knew what he was talking about. He had done it. He had been there and back.

In his career with the CIA, Harper had been the field executive in cases that Myers, the FBI desk jockey, had only read about. When asses got shot off, they belonged to the men who were actually in the action, not the staff scribes who kept notes in files and reminded the field agents of official policy and procedure.

So far, Harper had managed to keep his own ass intact, but that was because of his toughness rather than from not exposing it to fire.

They both knew that Myers would never be able to make the same claim. But he was a fair-haired boy, the big cheese in this interagency effort designed to show the world how the U.S. fights terrorism.

"Also," Myers continued, "I'll remind you that it isn't likely we'll lose him. Source One is as close as any spy could ever be. Hell, she's sleeping with the target nearly every night, for God's sake."

Harper shook his head stubbornly. "There's also a damned good chance she's been burned. And if that's so, she's dead meat the instant he decides to do her. That's another reason to snatch the guy while we can."

A flicker of doubt crossed Myers's face. When he spoke, his voice was harsh. "She hasn't been burned. That was all a panic without a cause. Nothing more."

Harper mentally collared his rising anger. "Look at the facts," he said. "One of our couriers drops out of sight. Disappears. Vanishes."

"He turned up," Myers interjected quickly.

"Yeah. Dead. And what's more—"

"*With* all his materials intact," interrupted the Bureau man. "The courier pak was still chained to his wrist. And I'll remind you it was still locked."

"It also gave every indication it had been tampered with."

"Negative. That was never proven. The only indications were external. The contents of the pak were undisturbed. And if it had been opened except under the proper light, they would have all been ruined.''

Harper looked at him incredulously. "And I suppose we're the only ones who would know that? That there's nobody in Russia or China or the Middle East who might also be aware of how to open it?''

"I'm not saying that, but . . .''

"Besides, look what happened afterward.''

Myers shifted in his chair and looked away. "We've been through that," he said stiffly.

As Harper thought it over, the evidence was overwhelming. Still, he struggled to make his voice sound reasonable, hoping it would keep Myers from just shutting off any consideration of his point.

"Hell, Jim, there were documents regarding three operations in that case. Within days, the other two dried up. Doesn't that tell you something?''

"Operations dry up all the time.''

"True enough, but . . .''

"All right, that answers it. It doesn't mean we were compromised.''

"But why those two?" Harper pressed. "Why not two others? You can't ignore the coincidence. For Christ's sake, we've started operations on less evidence than this. We ought to be able to stop one on it.''

Again a shadow crossed the Bureau man's face. As if to erase that shadow he leaned forward angrily, his voice rising. "That's exactly what it was—coincidence. Both those other operations were shaky to begin with.''

Harper dropped any attempt to reason with the man. "You're crazy," he snapped.

"Moreover, this operation didn't dry up, did it? Kadal didn't change his routine. He didn't vary one iota from what he'd told Source One he was going to do. He stuck to the plan. They're here in L.A., right on schedule, right like she said."

"So?"

"So that can only mean that he doesn't know about us. Whatever happened to that courier didn't involve Kadal. We were not burned!"

Harper knew it was a losing battle. He leaned back and shook his head grimly. "Take him out now, while we can. It's going bad. I can smell it. We're going to lose him, and get Source One killed in the process."

"Fuck Source One." Myers's face was ugly. "She knew the rules, and she decided to play."

"We're still responsible for her safety."

"Not legally responsible," snapped Myers. "We've played it by the book. If she eats it, that's just the way it is. We're in the clear. We'll fulfill our end, but beyond that, she'll have to take care of herself. She's a big girl."

"But she's not bulletproof," Harper said quietly.

THAT AFTERNOON, Harper made his approach to the safe house with unusual caution.

This was to be one of the rare face-to-face meetings with Source One. And, try as he might, Harper couldn't shake the feeling that something was about to go wrong. Perhaps as a result of this, he found a sense of reassurance in the familiar routines he used to detect possible surveillances from behind or ambushes ahead.

He switched cars. Now he was driving one he had never used before.

He made a sudden lane change from the fast lane of the Santa Ana freeway to the off ramp. He ignored the blaring horns from the other motorists. Instead, he checked the rearview mirror for similar maneuvers from behind, from somebody who might be following him.

Nothing.

He employed a half dozen other techniques, and each time the results were the same. He was clean.

The feeling was still there, though. It was an uneasiness, a vague fear that tightened his stomach and tingled in his arms and legs and lower back. Over the years he had trusted these instincts. Still, he couldn't help wondering if it meant he was losing his nerve.

Why me, he wondered for perhaps the hundredth time. Of all agents to get tagged for this kind of interdepartmental operation, why did it have to be Harper, the lone wolf operator of the Company.

And why Myers, for God's sake?

Not every FBI agent was a publicity-grubbing geek. There were a lot of good, hard-charging law officers

in the Bureau. There were even a few excellent ones.
But then, they wouldn't be the ones who got the nod
for a program like this—they were too busy doing their
jobs to bother with ass-kissing and politicking.

Myers, he knew, would never let his work interfere
with licking boot.

Myers, the career desk jockey, also had never been
face-to-face with a situation in which someone died
because somebody else got careless.

"Fuck Source One," Myers had said.

It was easy to talk tough about informants knowing what they were getting into. It was another thing
entirely to get the midnight call to come down to some
godforsaken place and see if some dead guy was
somebody you knew.

Harper knew. He'd gotten those calls.

Usually it was in the middle of a mission.

The rides in the police cars, the quiet scrutinies by
local cops and the morgues—Myers had never done
any of it.

Harper had.

He wondered why it was that the goddamned
morgues all seemed the same, reeking of the smells of
harsh chemicals and harsher death.

And then the ritual unveiling of the pitiful bastard
on the gurney. Unbidden, images of past occasions
surged before him, and for a moment he was there,
standing in some anonymous morgue. He could see it,
feel it—you clamped one mental hand on your throat
and the other on your guts and tried to stay expres-

sionless as the cloth was hauled back to reveal yet another instance of man's depravity.

"Jesus," he said aloud as he drove, "am I losing it?"

It was different every time, yet it was the same. There are only so many ways to systematically inflict pain on the body. Harper had seen them all, and always there was one dreadful common denominator—the pain in which the poor devil had spent his last hours or minutes of this existence.

Harper thought now of the woman they called Source One.

Her real name, he knew, was Laura Andrews. Real name was an overstatement; she was an actress, and this was her chosen stage title. She was an expatriate Jewish American who had drifted in and out of a dozen radical political causes before she had finally renounced both America and Israel and moved to Paris. Somehow she had drifted into contact with Fadi Kadal, and the experience had brought her full circle in her beliefs.

She loved Kadal, and she hated him. And in that peculiar nonlogic that women in general and actresses in particular seemed possessed of, she finally agreed to help destroy him.

Hence, her role as Source One.

As the CCA, or contact case agent—the agent who actually "ran" the source—Harper knew more about Laura than any other agent did. He could recite details about her life that she herself had likely forgotten. And, though he had only met her face-to-face on three occasions, he loved her.

More accurately, he was entranced, infatuated, obsessed.

It was utterly unprofessional, he knew. Moreover, he wasn't some dumb kid—the obsession was based on what he wished she could be, not what he knew she was.

Yet the feelings were there.

Harper hadn't breathed a hint of it to anybody. On a mission like this, he would certainly be yanked off the case. Conceivably, the operation would be scuttled entirely.

He gave a rueful snort. Well, that would be one way to get them to go with his suggestion and snatch Kadal while they could.

It also made him wonder if that was the reason he was so concerned with the safety of Source One. Had emotion clouded his experience and reason?

For the umpteenth time, he started to marshal the evidence, then said to hell with it.

The signs were there, and he was reading them correctly. This was more than just fretting—he had learned to trust his gut, and his gut said things were about to come unstuck.

A shape on a gurney, covered by a sheet.

For reasons that were largely unprofessional, he prayed that it wouldn't be Source One.

3

Fadi Kadal had some last-minute details to attend to.

A short man, his stocky frame running to plump from the culinary excesses of his jet-set life-style, Kadal looked like anything but the world's most accomplished assassin. Despite his physique, he looked urbane and strikingly handsome, with dark, lively eyes that sparkled in his brown face.

Behind the eyes lay a cold, malignant void that dispensed death without emotion whenever it suited him. He had never failed.

As a technician with the tools of his trade, Kadal was the best. An expert marksman with a rifle, he was an accomplished fighter with edged weapons, as well. In unarmed combat, his opponent was likely to discover that beneath the surface plumpness lay a surprising strength. He combined it with catlike reflexes, hours of training in the martial arts and a deep-seated sexual pleasure in inflicting pain, with deadly results.

His technical skills notwithstanding, Kadal's real abilities as an assassin lay in his extraordinary IQ and tactical genius. They kept him alive. They allowed him to kill, and kill again, despite the best efforts of teams of secret agents from several nations.

He could vanish as completely as if he had dropped off the face of the earth, even though anonymity would seem difficult to achieve given his Sybaritic tastes—indulging such a life-style would normally require at least some degree of exposure, even if only in exclusive circles. When Kadal was underground and in hiding, the agents around the world whose sole mission was finding him would receive tips and sightings of varying degrees of reliability.

With painstaking care, the leads would be tracked down, only to fade away.

During those times, word would periodically surface that Kadal was dead, that he had finally been taken out by somebody. Those stories served to further discourage the pursuers, and even the most cynical would begin to believe that this time, for once, it might be true.

Then a killing would occur that had all the Kadal earmarks, and it was back to square one.

Kadal looked at the two packages that had to be delivered. They were each placed in a standard, 1.5-cubic-foot cardboard shipping box.

He had packed them himself, carefully, painstakingly, almost lovingly. He had worn silk gloves, so there would be no chance of fingerprints. Not that it mattered; they would know who had sent them, anyway.

That was the best part of it.

Kadal took out a roll of brown filament tape. With precise movements, he taped the boxes securely shut. So craftsmanlike was his work that when he had finished, the two boxes looked identical.

Next he took out a yellow-bordered label of a local delivery and courier service called Speedy Drop. Same-day service guaranteed. For an extra charge, delivery would be made within the hour.

Kadal had paid the extra fee.

The boxes had to arrive that afternoon. Still wearing the silk gloves, he peeled off the waxed-paper backing from the labels, then smoothed the addresses onto the boxes. "Special Agent Jim Myers, Federal Bureau of Investigation."

He chuckled. Why do they always call themselves "special" agents, he wondered. Or, for that matter, why "safe" houses, he thought as he checked the labels again. However safe it had been, it wasn't now, thanks to the information that bitch, the American actress, had given him.

He felt a surge of excitement thinking about her. She had been reluctant, of course, but not for long....

That task done, he ran through his mental list one final time.

Everything was in order. The two boxes had been the last details, and now they were done, too.

"So," he said. "We are ready."

Nodding to himself, the world's most accomplished assassin prepared to go underground. Next stop—New York, four days from now.

4

"This damned waiting drives me crazy."

FBI Agent Julie Harris checked her watch again, the third time in ten minutes. She was a medium-sized, athletic young woman with dark hair that complemented her attractive face. Before joining the Bureau, she had earned a law degree at Notre Dame law school.

"Get used to it."

Harper's reply was curt. The vague disquiet he had earlier felt was now a massive depression. It settled over him and threatened to squash him flat. It was as if something in him had died, something vital, something that he couldn't live without.

The presence of the young Feebie—slang for FBI agent—didn't help any.

Julie meant well, he thought, and, sure, she was nothing short of beautiful. She was undoubtedly a hotshot in the finer points of constitutional law and suspects' rights. But she had a hell of a long way to go before she was any kind of counterintelligence operative.

"What's eating you, anyway?" she asked. "You still upset about that meeting?"

Harper regarded her coldly, then shook his head. "Nah, that's not it." He thought for a minute. "Ah, hell, to tell you the truth, I don't know what it is. I just have this feeling that things are about to come to pieces on us, and people are going to die, and nobody but me seems to feel that way."

"You worried about Source One?"

"Yes."

"You don't have some kind of crush on her or anything, do you?"

Harper's first impulse was to give a sharp look over at the young agent. Was it just an idle question, or was the kid more perceptive than she seemed? It took all his experience to restrain the urge. Instead, he turned toward her slowly.

Her look gave no clue. He summoned his best stage face and put on what he hoped was a rueful half smile.

"I probably wouldn't kick her out of bed, but that's about it," he said casually. "I guess I'm just concerned about all this 'hands off, catch him in the act' stuff. It's not my style."

"We have to do it that way for the courts," she reminded him.

"There are a lot of other ways to handle these things besides court."

"What? Assassination? Just kill him?"

Harper nodded. "Yeah. That's one way. Or just grab him and turn him over to the Israelis, or one of the other countries who'd like to get their hooks into him real bad. Let them do it for us.''

Julie looked shocked. "You can't be serious, Harper. That's murder. Or kidnapping, which is just as bad.''

"Yes, it is. It works, too.''

"But this is America, for God's sake.''

"Look. This guy's killed enough times that even in California they'd give him the chair. In three days he's going to try to do it again. And if he does, not only will those people die, but God knows how many others—including women and children—are going to eat it over in Beirut.''

"How do you figure?''

"Those people have been shedding blood forever, remember? And the Tri-Lateral Compact just might end all that. Maybe. It's the best shot we've got, anyway. And if it does, it'll be the greatest stride toward peace in this decade. Lebanon and Israel reaching an understanding at last. Muslims and Christians coexisting peacefully instead of killing each other's kids. The U.S. being big brother to both. It just might work, unless Kadal stops it.''

"Funny to hear you talking about getting peace by killing folks,'' Julie observed, deliberately twisting his words.

"Don't be an asshole,'' he said crudely. "I'm talking about stopping Kadal from killing folks.''

"Yeah. By killing him. Does that sound right?''

"Look at what just happened over there," Harper shot back. "Some Muslim fanatic just drove a truck bomb into a U.S. building in Beirut."

Her voice clouded in pain. "I saw it in the papers," she said quietly.

"It was supposed to be filled with a bunch of harmless translators. Civil servants and students. Instead, it was filled with even more harmless kids."

"I said I saw it. Don't keep reminding me of it."

He ignored her. "Unless you think the kids were secret agents of some sort."

"So what's your point?" Julie asked sharply. "What does that have to do with this? With America setting out to murder a man in cold blood, when we could be arresting him instead?"

"Are you telling me that if you could go back in time to ten minutes before that truck bomb went off, you wouldn't shoot that asshole in his tracks? Like the animal he is?"

She hesitated. "I don't know," she said simply. "I honestly don't know."

"Well, I know," he said curtly.

Julie thought for a moment. She was a strong, competent young woman, already well respected for her quiet abilities, even in an agency as traditional as the FBI. Harper had a point, she realized, and usually she was not one to shrink from doing whatever had to be done. To kill in self-defense was one thing, as it was to kill in the immediate defense of another.

But this was different, some sort of, well, *anticipatory* defense of others? Then a thought struck her, and she smiled wryly to herself—maybe we'll call it self-defense, the best defense being a good offense. But somehow it didn't sound right. Unwilling to let it die, she spoke up again.

"Anyway, even if we were going to do it your way, who'd we get to do it?"

Harper stared at her. "What do you mean?"

"Justify it however you like, you're still talking about murder," the young agent said heatedly.

"So?"

"Cold-blooded, premeditated murder."

"What's your point, Julie?"

"Who's going to do it? You? Or are you suggesting the Agency has an assassination division, staffed by beginning, intermediate and advanced killers? Just assign it to them?"

Harper laughed. "No, we don't have a division like that."

"Well, answer me," she persisted.

He shook his head. "Personally, I wouldn't mind doing it, and I could probably pull it off. But there are a few, uh, affiliated groups, not to mention any number of free-lancers, who could do it a hell of a lot better."

The young agent looked shocked. "You mean, you actually keep in contact with...with assassins, in case you need them?"

Harper's eyes narrowed. If she was this naive, or surprised, maybe he'd better not go any further with it, lest he find himself testifying before some American Civil Liberties Union-sponsored Congressional hearing someday.

"Nah," he said with a broad grin, trying to make light of the whole thing. "Hell, I'm just talking big, Jules. All woof, but no bite."

"Don't call me that," she said sharply.

He was aware that she was watching him closely. Her face was troubled and incisive at the same time. Something about the nickname had touched a nerve— an old lover's term of affection, perhaps?

But there was more. Behind it, she was watching him closely. Harper realized for the first time that she hadn't been simply debating with him.

She was fishing for information. Interrogating him, dammit, without him even realizing it. He looked her straight in the eye and winked; he reminded himself that she was one hell of a lot more perceptive than she appeared. Her next words confirmed it.

"No," she said slowly. "No, I don't think you're just talking big. Besides, I've heard a few things myself."

"What things?"

"Oh, names. Code names, probably." Her voice lost its accusatory tone as she probed her memory. "Black-bag groups the government calls in when nothing else will work."

"Like what?"

Julie wrinkled her brow. "Well, like...the only one I can think of is kind of strange. The Stone Group. It's something like that, anyway, but not exactly that. Stone Team? Stone Man? Yes, that's it. Stone man, stony man, something like that."

Harper shook his head. "Never heard of 'em," he lied calmly.

That did it, he thought. Never underestimate this woman again. She might be inexperienced—and naive—but she was definitely no dummy. Moreover, she just might make a hell of an intelligence agent some day, if she lived long enough. And could stop looking at her damned watch.

He let his thoughts drift to the name Julie had so fortuitously mentioned.

Stony Man Farm. It wasn't exactly common knowledge who they were, or what they were. But Harper had been around the netherworld a long time, and had heard bits and pieces over the years. And, from those scraps of information, he'd pieced together a fairly complete composite of the Stony Man Farm operation.

If anybody should be turned loose on Kadal, he thought, it should be some of those guys.

Harper knew that the government used Stony Man's operatives when the job didn't suit the in-house talent. That usually meant it was something the government wanted to disavow if it went sour, or something that was plain suicidal to begin with.

The two-tone chimes of the door bell jarred Harper back to his senses.

With a start, he realized that Julie had fallen silent while he was thinking. Predictably, she checked her watch at the sound.

"There she is." The young agent scrambled to her feet and headed for the front door.

"Hold it!"

"What?"

By way of reply, Harper grabbed an Ingram Model 10 submachine gun and slipped into the kitchen. It was a short, compact, utilitarian weapon, designed for close-in work. He covered the door as Julie moved to answer it.

She shot him a weary look and opened the door for Source One. Or, as Harper saw it, whatever enemy would be there instead.

"Afternoon, ma'am."

It wasn't Source One, and it didn't look like any enemy.

The voice belonged to a tall youth of maybe nineteen. He had very short, styled hair. His shoulders were wide but thin and lacking the meat that would come with full maturity. He wore khaki shorts and a yellow shirt on which was emblazoned Speedy Drop Courier Service. He held a couple of boxes, one on top of the other. Each was about a foot by a foot by maybe a little more than a foot. A clipboard rested on the top one.

Julie gaped. Finally she managed to stammer, "Yes? What is it?"

"Special delivery, ma'am. To Jim Myers, FBI agent, or his representative."

"He's not here." Already she had recovered. How in hell is this coming here, she wondered. This location is secret.

"Well, anyone can sign for it, as long as you're accepting it on his behalf." The youth set the boxes down and picked up the clipboard.

"What is it?"

The delivery boy shrugged. "Two boxes. Don't know what's inside. They're pretty light, though." He paused, then asked, almost shyly. "Are you with the FBI, ma'am?"

Absently, Julie nodded.

"Oh." The kid was impressed. "Well, would you like to sign for them?"

Confused, she picked up the pen and scrawled her name on the line. The youth tore off a copy and gave it to her.

"Where would you like these?"

"Huh? Oh, I'll take them." She reached out and the kid handed them over.

"Oh, yes. There's a letter, too." He held out a plain white envelope bearing the words "Mr. Jim Myers, Special Agent," and the address of the safe house. "You gotta sign for that, too."

She scrawled her name again, then shut the door as the kid withdrew down the walk.

His face grim, Harper strode from the kitchen and snatched the letter from her hands. He held it up to the light and saw that there was only a single sheet of paper in it. Furiously he tore it open.

"Hey," Julie protested. "That's not yours. And besides, what about fingerprints?"

"There won't be any."

He pulled the letter out. It bore a single typewritten line.

"They are not bombs."

Beneath the line was a single letter. K.

"Shit!" He spat the word out in a single, hate-filled snarl. Shoving Julie rudely out of the way, Harper grabbed the top box.

It was moderately light, considering the size of the box. Whatever the weight was, it was not spread evenly throughout the box so as to fill it. It seemed to be centered inside the box.

He twisted a dagger from his boot and sliced through the filament tape that sealed the top flaps down. Then he yanked the flaps up and looked inside.

The twisted white folds of a heavy clear-plastic bag lay inside. Mind on auto-pilot, he lifted it out, his eyes taking in the gruesome mass even as his mind was feeling its surprising weight and the fact that it was cold.

The skin had been removed, leaving the considerable meat and muscle that overlay the skull. The eyes were still there, as were the teeth. Both looked disproportionately large, without the eyelids and lips to frame them.

Julie put her hands over her mouth and made a gagging sound. She was normally not the sort to get queasy at the sight of a little blood, but this was different. Besides, the events of the past few days were taking their toll—a lot of pressure, little or no sleep.

She steeled herself. Then the morbid fascination of the tableau overcame her, and her mind recorded the events, scenes that she knew would stay with her forever.

Harper turned the grisly mass inside the plastic bag. His face was expressionless, a benign countenance that replaced his earlier anger.

The folds in the plastic distorted but did not conceal its gruesome contents. Crimson liquid caught in the creases and collected in the bottom of the bag. Through the transparent material, the eyes glistened a stark white in the midst of the meaty lump.

Harper gently replaced the bag in the box and turned to the second one. His dagger again sliced the filament tape. This box was full of Styrofoam packing chips. The CIA man reached in with both hands. He probed, then found what he was after.

The packing chips fell away as he withdrew another head.

Source One.

The head had been stuffed.

Julie watched in fascination as Harper gazed at the dark, vital face, fully preserved by the dreadful processes of the taxidermist's art.

The thick brown hair looked exactly as it had in life, worn straight and pulled back. The high forehead, the aquiline nose and cheekbones, the wide mouth—it was all there, skillfully caught by the process of preservation. Only the eyes were not quite right—the glass substitutes could never imitate the animated quality the actress had possessed in life.

Yet despite that, the eyes seemed to hold a special message as they gazed fixedly ahead.

Julie felt the room suddenly spin as a collage of images swirled before her.

"Harper was right," the face seemed to say. "You should have listened to him."

Julie shut her eyes in anguish. The images were still there.

"Fuck Source One," Myers had snarled. *"She knew the rules, and she decided to play."*

The room swirled giddily before her. As it did, Julie knew other things, too. Some of them were concepts that she understood for the first time. Others were glimpses from the future. The sensations overwhelmed her, and she sank to her knees in half a faint.

Harper *had* been right. She knew that now. "Wait and catch him in the act" wouldn't work with an enemy as evil as this.

And the blood. Death was everywhere. Blood seemed to cover the walls around her. She looked down; there seemed to be blood on her own arms. It ran down in rivulets and caught in the creases of her hands.

Some of the blood belonged to Source One. But there was other blood, as well.

The law had failed. The battle would have to be fought another way. In the swirling images, Julie saw Harper, dead. She felt the deaths of many others in the battle to stop the Lebanese monster.

Terror that was tangible washed over her. And through the blood and the fear, she saw a vision.

Three animal figures. At first she could not make out precisely what type of animals they were, in the mists of death that seemed to surround them.

Then she knew. They were lions. She discerned the biggest one first, its magnificent mane shuddering with every slow-motion step it took. On its flank were two other animals, heads occasionally rising from some kind of carcass that they were tearing apart. And the blood—it was everywhere.

In that moment, Julie knew she was looking at Death.

Death, and their only chance to stop their quarry.

Death was going to meet the killer. Blood would spill, and the only certainty was more killing.

How can you wash away blood with blood, she wondered.

Yet it had to be. The room spun faster, and Julie slumped to the floor in a faint.

A few feet away, Harper held the mounted head of Source One in his hands. With exquisite sadness, he brushed the lifeless cheek with his own lips in a single, light kiss. Then he replaced it gently in the box. Slowly, deliberately, he got to his feet, stepped over the prostrate form of the FBI agent and walked quietly out of the house.

5

"Haven't I kicked your ass enough, old man?"

The voice was mocking, taunting. Carl Lyons, about to bite a forkful of prime rib, looked up.

The challenger was Mike Schleigle, first-round draft choice at offensive tackle for the Los Angeles Rams. An All-American out of Michigan, Schleigle carried some 270 pounds of steroid-enhanced bulk on his six-foot-six-inch frame. Not much of it was fat. A good deal of it was in his neck, which when combined with his head, created the general impression that one of the Great Pyramids of Egypt was sitting on his shoulders.

Lyons sighed and laid his fork back on the plate.

It had not been a good day for the Ironman. Every fiber in his body ached. He was bone tired. Now, he just wanted to finish his prime rib, wash it down with a couple of beers and drag his carcass off to bed.

Somehow, given Schleigle's mood, it looked as if those things would have to wait.

In a way, this moment had been ordained some two weeks earlier. It all began during a workout in the weight room with John "Cowboy" Kissinger, newest man on the Stony Man team.

Lyons and Kissinger had been doing squats in a hole-in-the-wall power gym in Santa Monica, California. "Doing squats" for Lyons meant loading the Olympic bar up to 405 pounds—the bar plus four forty-five-pound plates on each end—and doing deep knee bends with the bar behind the neck, resting on the back of his shoulders. These were full squats, thighs breaking parallel to the floor. With every rep, the bar bent and flexed across the lifter's back from the massive weight on each end. At this point in the training cycle, they were doing "five by five."

Five sets of five repetitions per set.

That meant taking the bar off the power rack, gutting out a set of five squats and setting it back on the rack. Rest a couple of minutes, and do it again. Repeat the process five times.

Good for building strength, endurance, guts and for generally kicking your ass, as Lyons observed. Kissinger agreed, though an old knee injury compelled him to use about half the weight.

A newspaper lying around the gym carried an article on the National Football League spring training. It featured a batch of ministories on the key players drafted by the various teams.

"What a bunch of pampered, overpaid prima donnas," Lyons had observed disgustedly as he scanned the story while Kissinger was doing his set. He tossed the paper in the corner and stepped up to the power rack to wait for his turn.

The particular story he had been reading featured some all-American meathead out of Michigan who felt that $200,000 plus bonuses wasn't enough for a half a year's work for the Rams. His name was Mike Schleigle, and the paper discussed the state of his salary negotiations.

"It's an insult," Schleigle was quoted as saying. "I'd sure like to play for this ball club, but I honestly feel I'm worth more."

Howie Goldstein, his agent, agreed. "He'd rather not play at all than be insulted like that."

The picture in the paper showed Mike and Howie standing together with the stadium in the background. Both of them looked solemn and concerned.

Actually, the concern was genuine.

The meathead was worried that the negotiator for the team might take them at their word, in which case he could be forced to earn a living based on his skills. Two hundred thousand plus bonuses might be insulting, but at least it was better than minimum wage. Howie's concern was no less sincere; his agent's cut depended on the final figure he negotiated, and he had a life-style to maintain. Coke was expensive these days, and no relief in sight.

Lyons sweated out the last rep of his set and staggered forward to replace the olympic bar on the rack. Kissinger let him get out from under the weight, then tossed out the bait.

"They may be pampered and overpaid, all right, but they ain't prima donnas, Ironman."

Chest heaving, leaning forward with his hands braced above his knees to get his breath, Lyons shot his friend a disgusted look. "Bullshit. They're a bunch of spoiled brats."

Kissinger suppressed a smirk.

In the few months that Kissinger had been on the Stony Man team, he and Lyons had become fast friends. Cowboy Kissinger and Ironman Lyons. Both men were tough, and each respected the other's courage and abilities. But early on, the Cowboy—who had gotten his nickname in part from a freewheeling willingness to ignore rules and regulations whenever it suited him—had seen how easy it was to bait the brash Lyons.

Now he took delight in doing it at every opportunity. Rattle the Ironman's cage. Stir him a little and jerk his chain.

Kissinger gave an elaborate shrug. At six-two and two hundred pounds, he had a rangy, reckless, frontiersman air about him that somehow went with his nickname. "Hey, man," Kissinger said, "I agree. I'm just saying that, spoiled or not, they're good at what they're good at, which is going head to head with another goddamned buffalo. In that respect they're damned tough."

"That's a bunch of shit," Lyons snorted. "That's not tough. That's just a game."

"Maybe so," agreed the Cowboy. "But I've been there, and I know what it's like."

Lyons looked at him. Blond and blue-eyed, he was shorter than Kissinger, right at six feet. These days, thanks to the heavy lifting, he was weighing a solid 205, plus or minus. "What do you mean, you've been there?" he demanded.

"I played a year of pro ball with the Cleveland Browns after I got out of Ohio State. Believe me, friend, it's rugged in there."

"Oh, yeah? What did you play?"

"Wide receiver. I know how hard those boys can hit."

Lyon's eyes narrowed as he thought that over. He knew Kissinger was in fact one tough cowboy. That gave his words a credibility that went beyond what was written in any newspaper by some pro athlete groupie sportswriter.

Still, conciliation wasn't the Ironman's style.

"Whatever," he said with a shrug. "I played some ball in college myself, and I thought it was pretty tough until I grew up and found out what tough really was. Playing football is nothing. I'm just saying that in any real fight, they'd pop like a zit and fold like tissue paper."

"You played?" Kissinger asked. "What position?"

"Linebacker. What else?"

"Were you any good?"

Lyons grinned. He made an exaggerated flexing movement with his shoulders, a deliberate parody of macho. "What do you think? Look at me. Fast. Good lateral movement. Hard-hitting. I was awesome. Hell, I bet I could still kick some ass out there—right now— and I haven't even been training for it."

Got him, thought Kissinger. He began to reel in the line.

"I doubt it, buddy." He sighed with mock regret. "Times have changed. These dudes are bigger than ever before, and stronger. And we're not kids anymore. It's memory lane for guys like you and me."

"Crap. I've been fighting real wars since then, not some hyped-up game. That'll make up for a lot of size and age."

Kissinger grinned broadly and set the hook. "Carl, my friend, face it. Those young studs would knock your ass right in the dirt. You're a pro at what you do, but they're pros at what they do."

Lyons didn't reply, other than to make a show of flexing his neck muscles and checking them out in the gym mirror.

"Of course, if you would like to try," Kissinger had suggested casually, "I know a couple of guys with the Rams. In fact, one of their coaches was on Cleveland back when I was. We're still pretty good friends. He'd probably let us do some of the spring training with them."

Lyons was intrigued. "Think so?"

"Sure. In fact, I've done it a couple of years. Just for the conditioning and agility drills, of course. I bail out when the full contact stuff comes up. I could probably get you in, too."

As Kissinger spoke, Lyons cinched his lifting belt and stepped forward for another set of squats. "Might be fun at that," he observed. "Of course, I'd want to do the full contact stuff, too."

Kissinger smirked. "If you're up to it, that is," he said at the end of the set. "We could give it a try, anyway."

"Why not? We're between missions. We got nothing going. Might break the monotony."

"You want to?"

Lyons grinned his brash, Ironman grin. "Sure. Hell, yes. Line it up. Just make sure they understand I can't be responsible if I bust up a couple of their valuable prima donnas a little."

"I don't think that'll bother them."

A WEEK LATER, after taking a physical and being cleared by about a dozen doctors, Lyons and Kissinger showed up to practice. An overweight old trainer checked out their gear, gave them each a lock and locker and told them to report at six the next morning.

All locker rooms, no matter where, somehow felt alike, Lyons thought.

The same was true of police stations, morgues and the various government offices where Lyons had been briefed and debriefed during his Stony Man days. Now he felt a peculiar mixture of anticipation and nostalgia from the familiar locker-room sights and smells—the battered gray lockers, the white tile floors, the shower trees and over it all, the smell of stale sweat mingled with the pungent odor of liniments.

The trainer broke into his thoughts. "Oh, yeah, you gotta sign this." He shoved a sheaf of papers over at them.

"What is it?"

"It's a waiver and release of liability."

Lyons scanned the twelve-page document. It seemed to deal entirely with the fact that he wouldn't be able to sue the Rams if he got messed up in any one of a long list of ways. All the ways sounded painful. And if the contract was any indication, the Rams didn't seem too worried about Lyons hurting one of their valuable properties. For the first time, Lyons wondered if maybe he'd bitten off more than he could chew.

"Piece of cake," Lyons said jauntily. Grabbing the pen, he wrote his name in a disdainful scrawl on the last page. The old trainer was expressionless as he received the document.

That was eight days ago.

The first week—all seven days; no time off for weekends—had progressed from stretching and conditioning to light and moderate contact with pads. Today was the first day of full contact.

Kissinger bowed out from the full-hitting stuff. Over the week of relatively little contact, Lyons had forgotten his trepidations. Today he was back up to full cockiness.

"You sure you want to do this?" asked Kissinger. He had to admit he was impressed with how Lyons had handled himself so far. Still, up to now it had just been drill.

"This is what I've been waiting for," the Ironman said, moving his shoulders inside the pads. "It'll be a piece of cake."

Kissinger shrugged. What the hell, he thought, Lyons is a big boy. He can make up his own mind.

The real heavy-duty stuff came that afternoon. It involved a drill in which individual defensive personnel went up against two offensive players, a lineman and a fullback.

The play was intended to approximate the situation where the lineman had made a hole in the defensive line and was charging ahead with the ball carrier hard on his heels. In the real thing, the defensive backfield would be the only thing to stop the touchdown.

"Everybody got the picture?" barked the defensive coach. "This is the line of scrimmage, see." He pointed to the twenty-yard line on the practice field.

Lyons saw it. Adrenaline pumping, he was anxious to get to the hitting.

"We got the line of scrimmage," the coach repeated. "And we got a hole in the line. The offense just made a hole. You guys with me?"

They were.

"Offensive lineman is comin' through. Fullback right behind 'im. Defensive line is history. Now who's that leave?"

"Linebackers, Coach," volunteered one of the rookies.

"Yeah. That's right. Now the linebackers are here—" he pointed to a spot near the ten-yard line, some fifteen or twenty feet back from the scrimmage "—and they gotta stop the touchdown. Go through the blocker and get to the running back." He blew a sharp blast on his whistle. "All right! Let's move it! Linebackers down here and offense up by the twenty. Let's practice stopping the touchdown."

As Lyons saw it, the drill meant going one on two with a charging offensive lineman and the ball carrier. He tried to put Gadgets's words of wisdom out of his mind.

When Lyons got the nod, it was to go up against none other than Mike Schleigle, the All-American offensive tackle out of Michigan, and Otis Leon, a veteran running back. Schleigle, it seemed, had managed to overcome his scruples about taking a mere two hundred thousand a year, and had signed with the Rams. The camp watchers and sportswriters were predicting great things for him, even as a rookie.

Schleigle weighed in that morning at a svelte 268. The ball carrier, Leon, was lean at 210. For his own part, Lyons tried to forget that he had tipped the scale at only 205. He also tried to ignore what seemed like a decidedly amused quality the other players seemed to display.

They lined up, the two offensive men twenty feet from Lyons. One of the coaches called the signals.

"Ready! Set! Hut! Hut!"

At the second "Hut!" Schleigle and Leon exploded into motion. Two seconds later, the coach blew a short chirp on his whistle to signify that the offensive players were through the imaginary defensive line.

That meant it was up to the linebacker.

Lyons.

With the play in motion, trepidation vanished. The thrill of combat replaced it. With a week of agility and conditioning drills, plus a lot of good food, sleep and camaraderie behind him, on top of two months of heavy lifting, the Ironman felt strong and edgy and fast.

A triple high.

He surged forward.

The gap closed. The huge, meaty form of the All-American loomed before him like a buffalo. Lyons could see the face contorted in anger and determination.

The Ironman exploded forward with a second effort the instant before impact. Then, with a move that was nothing less than inspired, he shifted a few degrees to one side.

The result was that he made the hit just to the left of the big man's center, rather than straight on. The armored figures collided with a solid, meaty thud.

Simultaneous grunts of effort tore from their throats. Then the vectors of force worked in Lyons's favor, deflecting the charging lineman to one side.

Lyons, lower than his opponent, swept the hurtling form on past him, using both hands. Even so, the glancing impact jarred him down to his toes. For just an instant, blackness exploded in his senses. Then it vanished—a split second before he hit the rushing form of Otis Leon, hard on the heels of the lineman.

Lyons took him dead center in a letter-perfect tackle.

The Ironman's face landed squarely in the numbers, head up, so the cordlike muscles of the front of his neck would absorb the impact, arms wrapping around the charging fullback.

It was over in a second.

Lyons gradually became aware he was on the ground, his arms locked grimly around Leon's body. Some eight feet beyond them, Schleigle was also down. The play was over, and there would be no touchdown.

From somewhere a million miles away, Lyons heard the whistle.

A wave of spontaneous applause, whistles and catcalls ran through the assembled athletes. Those, too, sounded distant and surreal.

The jolt had knocked Lyons's system down to "barely conscious." He saw everything through a tunnel, his vision shut down to a narrow, straight-ahead field by the concussion. For some strange reason, he felt the prickle of the grass against his arms and against the calves of his legs below the nylon practice pants. He could smell the sweat of effort from his own and Leon's bodies. The only other sensation was a persistent ringing that forced itself into his ears.

Leon stirred. Lyons loosened his grip. Some part of his mind recorded, with a certain satisfaction, that the fullback was moving slowly himself as he got up. Then, his own mind still on auto-pilot, Lyons rolled to his knees and climbed stiffly to his feet.

Kissinger told him later that the play had caused a minor sensation among the other players. Even the fullback, Leon, had been impressed.

"Sign that dude," he'd said to the coach.

Lyons didn't remember any of it.

"And do you know what you said, you idiot?"

Lyons didn't.

"You gave that bullshit macho shrug and said . . ." He didn't finish, and instead just shook his head in amazement.

"All right, already. What?"

" 'Piece of cake.' "

The one man who had not been amused was Schleigle.

It was bad for his image to get his clock cleaned in front of God and everybody. As a highly touted—not to mention highly paid—rookie, he felt a certain professional pride was at stake. Accordingly, he devoted the balance of the afternoon to settling the score, in any way he could.

At first he tried the dirty tricks. Late hits. Low blows. A surreptitious gouge here and there.

Lyons could handle those. In fact, he had the advantage when it came to no holds barred. That was his kind of fight. For every cheap shot, the Ironman had a quick and painful response.

Even Schleigle soon realized this wasn't his turf. After that, he backed off from the in-fighting and concentrated on just going 110 percent on what he was good at.

The head-on-head drills.

Thus began one of the longest days of Carl Lyons's life.

Tough is tough, but the cold, hard fact—as Lyons was learning the hard way—was that 268 is a hell of a chunk bigger than 205. And since it would be outside the rules for Lyons to actually kill or cripple the young jock, or even to use any of the myriad pain-inflicting techniques he had learned at Stony Man, it meant a long time of spotting his opponent a lot of pounds.

By the end of the afternoon, several things had become clear.

Lyons was tougher than even Kissinger had imagined. Nobody should have been able to absorb the kind of punishment he had taken and still walk.

As for Lyons, he had revised his earlier views about all football players being prima donnas. They might be pampered and overpaid, but they were tough. The concept of knocking your ass in the dirt took on new meaning to the Ironman. He grew to understand it, to relate to it, to really *feel* it.

Yet when they called it quits that afternoon, Lyons had earned the respect of every man on the field. The hard way.

Schleigle couldn't stand it.

His inability to break Lyons, despite his best efforts, coupled with the ignominious defeat in the first play, galled him.

"I'm gonna kill you, old man." The All-American snarled the threat as they clomped up the cement ramp to the showers.

"Don't let the long walk over here stop you from trying," Lyons shot back sarcastically. "You know where to find me."

The tone of voice made Schleigle think better of undertaking an offensive at that time. He muttered something and lumbered on up the ramp.

"Watch that dude, man." The warning had come from Otis Leon as Lyons soaked his aching frame in a hot whirlpool. "He still thinkin' he owe you."

"Thanks, man."

Now, as Lyons tried to finish his prime rib, it looked as if Leon's prediction was about to be realized.

The Beef Barrel was heavy, dark furniture, red tablecloths, and, as the Cowboy put it, mondo food. Lyons was midway through a max cut of prime rib when he became aware of Schleigle standing across the table.

"Yeah, old man, I'm talking to you. Haven't I kicked your ass enough already?"

Lyons looked up at the oversize young man. Then he shook his head disgustedly and turned back to the rib.

"Hey, you! You hear me?" Schleigle's voice boomed. The room fell silent as the background conversation came to an abrupt halt.

"Ah, shit," Lyons muttered to his prime rib. Then he slowly raised his gaze again. "I hear you," he said evenly.

"Well, I'm tired of your face, old man. What do you think about that?"

"Good for you."

The All-American's jaw jutted angrily. "In fact, I think I'm just gonna whip your ass for you. How's that sound?"

Normally, Lyons made it a rule never to fight except in the line of business. Those times it was unavoidable. But this was different. Maybe it was because the week of football had gotten him thinking back in the mode before he had learned that fighting was meant for survival only. Whatever the reason, he welcomed the chance to take a shot at the giant jerk without being bound by the rules of football.

Deliberately, the Ironman ignored the taunt.

Turning back to his dinner, he cut another piece of prime rib and speared it with his fork. He spread horseradish on it and popped it into his mouth, chewing slowly and knowing it was antagonizing Schleigle.

"Hey!" The voice boomed angrily. "I'm talkin' to you, boy!"

Lyons looked up and paused in his chewing. "Which is it?" he said around the beef.

"Huh?"

"First, it's 'old man,' and now it's 'boy.' Seems like it can't be both, somehow."

Behind them, somebody snickered.

Schleigle's face contorted in rage. He bent swiftly down and swept the red tablecloth and contents off the table. At the shattering crash, the hostess in the foyer reached for the telephone and dialed 911.

Lyons resumed chewing his rib.

"You're dead, asshole!" bellowed Schleigle.

Lyons slowly finished chewing and swallowed. Then he set the fork carefully on the polished tabletop, now that the cloth was gone. When he spoke, his voice was low, almost soft.

"Fuck you."

An unintelligible roar escaped from Schleigle's throat. He reached down and grabbed Lyons with both hands by the shirtfront, preparing to haul him across the table.

Combining principles of aikido and street fighting, Lyons went with the movement rather than opposed it. Rising, he stepped quickly on the seat of the heavy chair and drove forward with all the strength on his legs, slamming his forearm into the man's throat. Even as he did so, he heard a low warning from Kissinger.

"Don't kill him, Ironman."

Schleigle made a noise somewhere between a gag and a grunt. He staggered backward from the impact, then lost his footing and sat down heavily.

Lyons stayed roughly on his feet. He ended up half standing, half crouched above the huge lineman. Curling his fist, he struck two short, sharp blows. Schleigle's head snapped backward, then Lyons danced away and waited.

He didn't have to wait long. The All-American drew a raspy breath, then rolled to his feet and plunged headlong after the Ironman.

Lyons's fighting technique had once been described as "lower Broadway brawl," referring to a particularly bad area he had patrolled as a cop. It combined bits and pieces from several martial arts disciplines, mixed with "mad-dog mean" and "psychotic frenzy" where appropriate.

Still, somewhere along the line, he had studied aikido, and used those movements for much of his close-in fighting. The idea was to go with, not against, the forces directed against you by your opponent. That was the circle concept that underlay aikido—coming on around and using the enemy's own energies against him.

When Schleigle launched into his tackle, he was committed. There was no changing direction. Lyons stepped quickly to one side and snapped both hands onto the man's forearm. Then he turned into the direction of Schleigle's plunge. Throwing his weight into it, he levered the young giant headfirst into the wall.

Wood paneling splintered. The building shook with the crash of 268 pounds of Lyons-assisted impact.

The big man dropped to his hands and knees. Blood flowed from a split in his forehead. Dazed, he moved his head slowly from side to side, grunting like a bull.

"All right, Mikey, baby, fun's over."

Lyons's voice was cold. He moved up on the All-American and twisted his wrist into a scientific hold that allowed him to control the amount of pain.

He applied the pressure. With a grunt, the still-dazed jock tried to move away from the agony until the wall stopped him. Then he couldn't go any farther, and ended up half lying, half kneeling against the wall near the floor. His cheek was pressed against the ruined paneling, one arm twisted back and secure in the Ironman's grip.

"Now listen to me, Mikey. And listen hard. You been acting rude, man. Real rude. And it's gonna stop. You know why it's gonna stop, Mikey?"

Schleigle didn't respond.

Lyons increased the pressure on the wrist. "Answer me, Mikey!"

The big man grunted in pain. "All right, all right."

"It's gonna stop because if you come at me again, I'll break you into pieces. You read me?"

Schleigle nodded. His cheek left dark smears of blood against the paneling.

"Good. Now listen to me some more, Mikey. You're big and strong and on the ball field, you're tougher than I am." Lyons paused. Nobody said anything. He took a deep breath and continued. "There. I said it. On the ball field, you're tougher. Does it make you feel better?"

Without really waiting for a response, Lyons went on.

"You're tough, but you're a bully. I don't like bullies. The world doesn't like bullies. And once in a while, a guy comes along who's not gonna put up with that bullshit.

"Well, that guy just came along. Me. And off the field, where there's no rules and no pads, you don't stand a chance. I'll take you every time.

"You come at me unarmed and I'll put you in the hospital. You come at me with a weapon, and I'll put you in the morgue. Believe it. It's what I do."

The room was silent. Lyons felt his anger receding. In its place came embarrassment. He released the big man's wrist and rose to his feet. For a moment he stood and regarded Schleigle grimly.

Sirens wailed in the distance. Then Kissinger was at his side. "Uh, nice speech, Ironman. But maybe we better think about easing on out of here."

Lyons nodded. Self-consciously, he made his way to the door. None of the other players made any move to stop them.

As they neared the door, a voice called them back.

"Say, Ironman." It was Otis Leon, the fullback. His voice wasn't hostile. A lazy half smile split his black face.

"Yeah?"

"What *do* you do, man?"

Lyons saw his expression and grinned. "Pest control, man."

Leon thought for a moment, then wrinkled his brow. "You a killer, dude? A hit man?"

Lyons didn't respond.

The All-Pro remained silent for a moment, then he raised a clenched fist. "Right on," he said enthusiastically. "You be cool, man."

Lyons returned the salute. "Right on." They vanished into the darkness.

6

"Put it in words of one syllable, amigo," said Rosario Blancanales with an easy grin. "Who wants to do what to who?"

"Whom," corrected Hal Brognola, Chief of Operations for Stony Man Farm, with a wink.

"Whatever. I just want to know who the players are and how they line up. It helps in figuring out who to kill."

"Whom," corrected Brognola again.

"Huh?"

"Not 'who to kill.' It should be 'whom to kill.' Get it right, will you?"

Blancanales rolled his eyes in mock exasperation. Nicknamed "The Politician," or simply "Pol," Blancanales was a broad-shouldered, athletic man in his forties. The son of illegal aliens, Blancanales had grown up in the barrios of Los Angeles and San Diego. Then, when Vietnam had come along, he had joined the Army to defend the country that at the time regarded his parents as "wetbacks" or "illegals."

Intelligent and quick-witted, Blancanales had volunteered for Special Forces. The stunning hardships of Jungle Warfare School and Jump School had broken a lot of good men while it case-hardened others.

The Politician had been in the latter category. In the Asian hellgrounds he had become a seasoned warrior, possessed of both the mind and the skills necessary for it.

Yet for all his lethal skills, Blancanales was on the surface a gregarious and easygoing charmer, able to fit into any group with a smile and a wink. Minutes after meeting him, men liked him and women speculated about being in bed with him. His forehead was deeply lined, his black hair and mustache streaked with startling gray.

Before the sudden and urgent call to "Report now" to Stony Man Farm, Blancanales had been alternating between ball-busting workouts and trying to eat his way through every Mexican and Italian restaurant in San Diego.

The results were impressive. He was in the best shape of his life, carrying a solid 180 pounds on his five-foot-eight frame. On most men, this would have looked blocky, but on Pol the effect was somehow mitigated by his natural grace.

To Blancanales's right in the Stony Man conference room that morning sat Hermann "Gadgets" Schwarz. Able Team's electronics whiz and resident genius grinned and muttered, "Who. Whom. Who. Whom. Guy sounds like a goddamned owl."

Brognola beamed and nodded, chewing on his inevitable cigar. He recognized the banter as a release of sorts, a shared recognition of the fact that the only reason they were together was that something had come unstuck, and Able Team had to either put it back together or pick up the pieces.

There was also the unspoken but shared understanding that these jobs always meant danger, laying it *all* on the line, and every one of these meetings could damned well be the last one.

It had become a familiar ritual. Premission syndrome, Gadgets had once called it.

So far, they'd always made it. Everybody had managed to be there for the "next meetings," no matter how dirty or dangerous the last mission. They'd survived. But the inevitable question lurked in the back of the minds of each—do the odds get longer against you because you beat them last time, and the time before that and the time before that, as well?

Brognola had once tried to voice that concept at one of these meetings. Blancanales had seized on it immediately.

"You mean, is it like there's somebody keeping score? Somebody 'up there?' Some kind of cosmic score sheet on us?"

Brognola nodded. "Exactly. Every time we—you guys, actually—somehow make it through a tight one, do the chances get slimmer for the next time?"

"Yes," said Blancanales. "It has to be that way. It's the only way that makes sense."

"No," said Gadgets simply.

"Why do you say no?" inquired Brognola, intrigued.

Gadgets shrugged. "According to the laws of probability, in a pure chance situation, what happened before has no effect on the next time. You toss a coin twenty times and get twenty heads, it's still fifty-fifty on the next toss. It doesn't get slimmer, even though it seems like it should."

"But is this a pure chance situation?" persisted Brognola. "Or is this something else, something where what happened before affects what happens next?"

Seeing the uncomfortable silence that followed, Brognola mentally kicked himself. Why did I mention this, he wondered. Here I'm talking about ropes to a bunch of guys who damned well may be on the way to their own hanging!

Finally Blancanales spoke again, his voice soft and distant. He stared into space ahead of him, his gaze unfocused as he tried to put his thoughts into words.

"Yes, amigo, I believe it is not pure chance. Death is a real thing. It waits for each of us, and that is right. But we—" he hesitated and for once had to search for the words "—we taunt death. And I believe that he knows it, and he will make it harder for us each time."

Lyons didn't like what he was hearing. He didn't like any of it. He tossed out a sarcastic reply in an awkward attempt to lighten the mood.

"Pisses him off, you mean? Good. I hope so. It's good for him."

"Who?"

"Death. The cosmic scorekeeper. Whoever the hell you guys are talking about."

Not to be deterred, Blancanales nodded seriously. "We're gamblers. We bet our lives. And every time we win, he remembers. He's all the more determined to win the next time."

Lyons made a disgusted pushing motion with his hand, as though waving away the idea.

"Ah, fuck that," he said curtly, deliberately crude. "There's no goddamn cosmic scorekeeper."

"How so?" queried Brognola.

Lyons gave an angry jerk to his head. "You shoot better than the other guy, you win. You don't, and you lose. It's just that simple. I don't have time for that heavy cerebral shit. It's more important to practice shooting."

The vehemence with which he spoke belied his words.

Brognola, wisely, had let the subject drop without further debate. But now that the question had been framed, it would always be there at these premission briefings, like a lover's indiscretion, foolishly confessed when silence would have been better.

It was there today, in the conference room at Stony Man Farm, underlying the deliberately light banter over the Politician's grammar. And this time, it was Lyons—the Ironman himself—who felt it so strongly. His mind was filled with thoughts of death and long odds, largely because of the dream he had about the blackjack game with Death.

Now, in the cold light of day, the dream had faded. But it had left its mark on him, and as he waited with the others for the meeting to get under way, the Ironman's mind was filled with the realization that Death was there, waiting.

Of course, it was only a dream.

Still, as dreams go, it had been a bitch. Damn that Brognola anyway, he thought, him and his question about the odds getting longer against you with every mission.

At that moment, the telephone in the Stony Man conference room rang. Brognola swiveled in his chair and answered it. He listened for a few moments, nodded and ended with a businesslike, "Got it. Thanks."

Turning to the three men of Able Team, he said, "Let's get started. We're supposed to be joined by a couple of other people, but they'll be late. In the meantime, I'll give you the background."

Good, thought Lyons, now we can get down to work. He pushed the dream—and Brognola's question about the odds—from his mind.

As he called the small meeting to order, Brognola assumed his customary position at the head of the table.

On the outside, he was a burly, affable man, with a fondness for good cigars, which he smoked or just carried around unlighted. Formerly head of a covert operations section of the Justice Department, Brognola was the Chief of Operations for Stony Man

Farm, and liaison between the Farm and the Oval Office.

The "Head Fed," as everyone called him.

A long walnut table dominated the conference room. Apart from the table, everything in the room was standard U.S. Government issue. The walls were government-approved beige, the carpet a sturdy brownish-orange nylon that seemed indestructible— "good for areas of heavy foot traffic like hallways or for landing aircraft on," as Gadgets Schwarz, Stony Man's resident comedian, had once put it.

Even the clock was standard—in this era of digitals, the timepiece over the door was a plain, round clock with black hands and a red sweep second hand. It looked like a million other clocks Lyons had seen in a million other government buildings, police stations, courthouses and morgues.

Stony Man Farm was founded on the premise that the law was basically good and worked reasonably well most of the time to control the greed and the evil inherent in all men.

But there were some whom the law could not touch, men for whom the law actually served as both a sword and a shield.

To these criminals, the law became a shield because they hid behind legal technicalities; it was a sword because in some cases they used the law as a tool of crime, buying politicians and judges and obstructing investigators by frivolous countersuits and claims of harassment.

The evil lay in the fact that when it was over, the little guy was the one who got the shaft.

Carl Lyons knew. Rosario Blancanales and Gadgets Schwarz knew. And because they knew, and didn't like it, Able Team existed.

In the final analysis, that was what the Stony Man Doctrine was all about. Stopping the predators. Fighting, and if necessary, dying for other people, people you never met. Most of them would never know of your existence, let alone your sacrifice.

So why do it? What's the use? Who cared?

Every man on the team had asked himself these questions a thousand times.

And, for every man on the team, the answers always came up the same. It was simple to understand, and it was impossible to explain.

You did it because it was right.

Today, in the Stony Man conference room, Brognola opened a leather note pad as he called the small meeting to order. Notes covered the yellow legal papers inside. Cigar held loosely between the index and middle finger of his left hand, he scanned the writing, making an occasional notation with the gold pen he held in the other hand. Finally he spoke.

"I'll get started with the background information. There are a couple of FBI agents who're supposed to be here—that's what that call was about—but I've been told they've been delayed."

Lyons, Blancanales and Gadgets were the only others in the room. They lounged at various positions around the long table. At the mention of the FBI, Lyons rolled his eyes.

"Typical Bureau," he said disgustedly. "What happened? They have a bank robbery they had to go check out while this matter of national security waits?"

Brognola deflected the criticism. "Plane trouble. They're coming from L.A. Had to be rerouted through Atlanta. That's hardly anything the Bureau can control."

"They could have started sooner. Taken an earlier flight," Lyons persisted.

"Not when the crisis pops up yesterday afternoon, the President gets told last night and the order goes out to be here this morning. Be reasonable, Ironman."

"Why?" But Lyons grinned as he said it.

"Who are the agents?" inquired Blancanales. "Anybody we've worked with before? Or some f.n.g.s?" He used the unofficial military term, the initials meaning "fucking new guys."

Brognola grinned. "Nobody we've worked with, as far as I know. Real good, though, I hear. Definitely not your standard Bureau clones."

"We'll see," muttered Lyons, wondering what Hal seemed to be smiling about.

When Brognola began speaking again, his tone signaled it was time to get down to business.

"It's called the Tri-Lateral Compact," he began. "Ultrasensitive, and, as a result, Code Red. Beyond

Top Secret. Shred your ears after you've heard what I'm about to tell you."

"Aren't they all?" muttered Lyons, rubbing his neck. He had never realized that so much stiffness and pain could be centered in one part of his body, a legacy from eight days of spring ball with the Rams.

Brognola ignored him. "We're talking about the Middle East. Lebanon, to be exact. Beirut."

Blancanales let out a low whistle. "Now that's an assignment. We ought to be able to find some action there, all right."

"You won't be going there. Not at this point, anyway. But it's what this job is all about." Brognola took the unlit cigar from his mouth, looked at the soggy end, then stuck it back between his teeth. "We're talking a religious war, which is important only because it explains how deep and how bitter the hatred is. And how important the mission is.

"Basically, we've got Muslims and Christians. There's enough hatred there to keep people killing one another for the next hundred years."

"Unless?" prompted Blancanales.

"Unless the Tri-Lateral Compact goes through."

"What is it?"

Brognola gave a slight shrug. "A treaty of sorts. It'll set up a government that will allow the Muslims and the Christians to come to terms. Maybe not be the best of friends—that's sometime off—but at least stop blowing up one anothers' kids."

At the words, a shadow passed over Lyons. He remembered a small village in South America. He saw again the butchered women and children, good and honest people who had died because of the power lust of greedy politicians and generals. Perhaps the only deaths the Ironman couldn't shut his mind to were those when kids died in the indiscriminate carnage wrought by their parents.

The rows of plain wooden coffins as the survivors picked up the pieces were etched into his memory. He remembered the stoic anguish of those who were still alive, outwardly dignified, while inside their hearts broke.

It had struck him how pathetically, helplessly small a child's casket is. And, he thought bitterly, we've got thirty-two more of them now, over in Beirut.

"So tell us about the Tri-Lateral Compact," said Lyons, his voice cold and angry.

"As I said, you've got two main groups, the Muslims and the Christians. They've been fighting for years. Then in 1982, the Israelis invaded Lebanon, during part of the struggle against the PLO.

"At first, the Muslims saw the Israelis as liberators who had freed them from the PLO. But as time went on, friction developed, and the Israelis became just another occupying force to the Muslims."

"That's when they started killing one another," Blancanales observed.

Brognola nodded. "Basically, yes. One of the Muslim factions, the Shiites, were the most radical.

And bloodthirsty. They saw themselves as the bottom dogs, and it was a hell of a big dog-pile, at that. So they started doing what groups like them have done everywhere."

"You mean killing innocent people," said Lyons.

"Probably. Killing, for sure. They got arms from Syria and Iran. They got tactics and philosophy from the Ayatollah Khomeini. They learned terrorism, modern-style. And they found out they liked it.

"Truck bombs killing U.S. Marines in Lebanon, kamikaze-style. Hijacks. Most recently, a bunch of school kids. Wholesale and selective death."

Nobody spoke for a few moments. Finally, Gadgets broke the silence, his voice quiet and somehow tired. "So where do we fit in? Short of nuking the place, we'll never stop it."

"Maybe. Maybe not. That's where the Tri-Lateral Compact comes in. We're starting to see indications that even the Shiites are getting a little concerned at the escalation of the festivities. Right now, though it's close, it looks like even the Shiites are willing to support the Compact."

"So how does this involve us?" asked Lyons, echoing the sentiments expressed by Gadgets. It sounded more like a diplomatic matter than something for Able Team.

"As I said, it's close. There's still a strong faction that wants total war. The one thing they don't want is the Tri-Lateral Compact to go through."

The others thought that over.

They knew the type, of course. The objectors would be the fanatics, the twisted revolutionaries who existed to feed their own hatred. Not that there was anything wrong with that, of course, as long as they only killed themselves and others like them.

But it didn't work that way in real life. The inevitable result of this terrorism was the death of innocents, the shattering of lives other than their own. It was the consummate selfishness.

Brognola looked at them.

"The final session in preparing the Tri-Lateral Compact is due to take place in three days. In New York. As I said, it's been kept under wraps, even from the media."

"Who's going to be there?" asked Blancanales.

"It's expected to be the final session. If all goes well, it'll be prepared and signed a couple of weeks after that. That means the big guns will be there for this one." He drew in a long breath. "The President of the United States. The Prime Minister of Israel. Leaders of the Lebanese Muslims. All in one room, hashing out the final details of the Compact. We're talking Nobel Peace Prize caliber if this goes through."

The outline of the threat was starting to materialize to the three men of Able Team.

"And somebody doesn't want it to go through," said Blancanales slowly.

Brognola nodded.

"And if I didn't want it to go through, and I wanted to make a big splash at the same time..." continued

Blancanales. He stopped, and let the sentence dangle unfinished.

Brognola nodded.

"Do we know who?" Lyons asked.

Brognola nodded. "That's where we—and specifically, you guys—come in."

At that moment, the door to the conference room opened, and FBI Agent Julie Harris walked in.

7

"Not your standard Bureau clone," Brognola had said. That had to be the understatement of the year.

She was beautiful.

With a practiced eye, born of years of cop experience and girl-watching, Lyons noted the physical data. Five-six. Maybe five-seven. Say, 125, all of it, well, *tight* was a good word, like an athlete. A good tan. Hair, dark brown, no curls, thick but worn moderately short in a dramatic, almost wild, modern style.

But the stats didn't tell the story. They never did. In his early years as a cop, Lyons had recorded thousands of descriptions from thousands of witnesses. He knew too well how inadequate language was to paint the picture of the person.

Especially here. The woman who entered the room had a compelling vitality about her. It seemed almost tangible. It was a strength of sorts, a quiet confidence. Intelligence. Ability. Trenchancy without arrogance.

Don't *ask* me if I can handle it, she seemed to say. Just give me the job and I'll *show* you.

Lyons did not consider himself easily swayed by feminine good looks. That was especially true when the woman was trying to do what he regarded as a man's job. Something like being a cop, a steelworker, a fireman or a lumberjack. Or a secret agent, except in cases where seduction was required, and even then, the woman was essentially one of the props.

In his book, it was a question of ability, period. Not mental ability, but physical, down-and-dirty, fighting-for-your-ass ability. Ability that damned few women had.

"We don't make pro basketball teams hire a quota of women," he had once argued to a lieutenant at L.A.P.D. "We don't make pro football teams do it, either. And why not? Because they can't do the rough stuff. Not like a man. So why does the P.D. have to hire women cops to be my partner when I'm trying to break up a bar fight in some goddamned outlaw biker bar?"

The lieutenant had looked at Lyons. "Are you saying there's no woman in the world who could take you?" she had asked coldly.

Lyons's jaw had clenched, but he had dodged the question. "Maybe. Maybe not. And I'm not saying there aren't jobs on the P.D. they can handle. But on the average, they can't cut it when it comes to march-or-die time."

"And men can?"

Lyons had shaken his head. "Other things being equal, a bigger person will take the smaller person every time. Most men are bigger and stronger than most women. That's all."

"I'd suggest," the lieutenant had replied icily, "that you confine your little theories to the locker rooms and the bars. *Officer* Lyons."

Only two women had ever met Lyons's standards as a partner in war. He had loved them both, in quite different ways—one as a sister, the other completely, as a lover, a part of himself.

Both were dead.

The "sister," April Rose, had died in the defense of Stony Man Farm. The lover, Flor Trujillo, had died when an RPG rocket took out the helicopter she was riding in....

Yet despite it all, when he saw FBI Agent Julie Harris for the first time, all Lyons could think of was "Golly!"

He turned to Blancanales and whispered, "Very nice, but can she shoot?"

It was a schoolboy wisecrack. He said it to conceal the impact that her beauty, and her presence, had on him. And maybe there was another reason, something he hadn't done since he was in high school—to show off.

She heard him, because as she moved to the head of the table where Brognola was getting to his feet, she tossed out a quiet response that was half answer, half challenge.

"Well enough."

Blancanales whistled softly between his teeth. Gadgets grinned. Lyons, taken aback at the prompt reply, was saved from any further embarrassment by Brognola.

"Gentlemen, this is Agent Julie Harris of the FBI." He introduced each of them in turn, then asked her, "Is Agent Myers coming, too?"

She shook her head. "He got called off. Right when we landed. He was told to report to main headquarters. I'm it."

Brognola nodded and gestured to a chair. "Have a seat. I understand you're going to fill us in on the target."

Before being seated, she opened a black briefcase and took out a manila folder. She extracted two page-sized photographs and slid them along the table.

Lyons reached for one of the pictures. It showed the face and shoulders of a man with dark hair. Mideastern, he thought. Probably Lebanese, based on what Hal was saying earlier.

"His name is Fadi Kadal," she said mildly. "He kills people. He's very good at it." She hesitated and took a breath. "I'm supposed to ask you to kill him."

Lyons studied the photo.

The face was handsome. The shape of the head was essentially square, with the forehead accented by wavy black hair. The lips were thick and fleshy—Lyons had heard some women say they found that sexy, though why that would be so was beyond him.

Maybe that was a good thing, he had decided.

But there was something else about the face that struck him. In an irrational way, it made him hate the man. Without any more to go on than his instincts and a black-and-white surveillance photo, Lyons knew this man would be a complete, unmitigated enemy, the consummate foe.

The face projected a sort of animalism and a cruel licentiousness.

It showed in the eyes and in the set of the mouth. Here was a man given to excesses—going to the extreme in everything. In eating, Lyons was certain, he would revel in the richest foods and wines. In sex, he would be cruel; inflicting pain and fear would be his aphrodisiac. In his chosen profession—murder—he would take too much delight. He would kill with an unwholesomeness, a corrupt and probably sexual pleasure. Killing would be the ultimate subjugation of another.

This guy would go in for necrophilia, given the chance.

Whoa, Ironman, he told himself. You're reading a hell of a lot into a single goddamned snapshot. Maybe you're getting too old for this shit. Or, he wondered ruefully, maybe there was something about this female Fed that was getting to him already.

But there was something else about the face, something he couldn't quite put his finger on. For some reason, he thought of the dream, death's bony fingers turning over the cards one by one. But that wasn't it, exactly; whatever it was lurked in the recesses of his mind, just out of reach.

To hell with it. It would either come to him, or it wouldn't. Get on with the program.

He slid the photo down to Blancanales.

Lyons realized he was getting restless. He needed a mission. It had been too long. Too much cerebration and not enough action. Playing ball with the Rams had been okay for a while, but even that had lacked something. The indefinable edge hadn't been there, the thing that kept him coming back even though it gave him dreams of death.

The ultimate gamble. Challenging the odds with nothing to bet except your life. And it was a ridiculous gamble, at that. You never won anything that you didn't already have. Winning was just not losing. Yet. And losing was death, or worse—death preceded by mind-exploding agony.

It was all he could do not to start pacing the room. Come on, guys, let's get on with the program, he thought impatiently.

"All right," he said to Julie with faked casualness. "You want him killed. Piece of cake. It doesn't sound like standard Bureau procedure, but if that's what you want, and what he wants—" Lyons gestured at Brognola "—no sweat."

For a moment, she didn't respond. Then she gave a little apologetic smile. "No, it's not standard Bureau procedure."

She thought of her debate, or argument, with the CIA man, Harper, on the subject of preventive homicide. What an irony that here it was she who was conveying the request now that things had gone to hell.

"But?" prompted Blancanales.

"We tried other ways. They didn't work. The orders came down. Stop him. Whatever it takes. I guess they think you guys are what it takes."

"The Tri-Lateral Compact?" inquired Gadgets.

She nodded. "Yeah. He's going to kill everybody involved in the conference, unless we—you—can stop him."

"And that's when?"

"Three days from now."

They thought it over. A treaty that could bring an end to centuries of bloodshed in the Middle East. Heads of state, including the President of the U.S., gathered to sign it. And the man in the picture dedicated to causing their deaths.

"Any reason why they can't just change plans?" asked Gadgets.

"What do you mean?"

"Move the location of the meeting. Delay it a couple of days. Make it take place in the middle of a ring of tanks. Hell, anything like that."

FBI Agent Julie Harris shook her head slowly. "That was suggested. The President nixed it."

"Why?"

"It's kind of complicated, actually. The way it was explained to me was that the Tri-Lateral Compact was shaky at best." She paused.

"Go on," urged Blancanales.

"Well, one of the things necessary for it to get ratified is for the U.S. to make a show of stability and security. Admitting we have to move it or change it for security could be just enough to scuttle the treaty."

It was Blancanales who spoke. "If everybody gets blown away, that'll scuttle it for sure."

Julie shrugged. "That's true. The President has apparently decided to do it this way, though."

Blancanales shook his head. "Dangerous game he's playing—"

"It's his choice," Lyons interrupted. "Do you have any information on how Kadal is going to go at this?"

She shook her head. "Not really. We know the methods he likes to use. We know what he's used in the past. But beyond that, we're just guessing."

Lyons grimaced. It wasn't much to go on. Aloud, he said, "So tell us how he's done it in the past."

"He's an expert at the hand-to-hand stuff. Knives and unarmed combat. They say he's as strong as a bull, and utterly unstoppable in a fight. But of course those things aren't exactly suited to a mass assassination."

"Bombs?" inquired Gadgets.

"He's used them before, though our sources say he doesn't like them. He likes his hits to be more personal. Torture is his favorite, apparently, but it's hardly suitable here.''

Lyons nodded to himself. That fits the picture, he thought, recalling his hunches about the photograph. The kid could still call 'em. Maybe he wasn't too old for this, after all.

He thought something else, as well. Agent Harris, he realized, had really great legs. And as long as he was on the subject, the area north of the equator, the northern hemisphere, so to speak, looked just as spectacular.

Or maybe it should be ''hemisphere*s*,'' he thought, amused. That's it, he decided—she has great northern hemispheres. Sounds better than boobs, somehow.

''So how's his favorite way?'' Pol was prodding the young agent. ''For something like this, that is.''

''For most paid killings, he likes the good, old-fashioned rifle bullet. Long range. Selective. Personal.''

''Reach out and touch someone,'' Gadgets quipped with a wink.

She gave a start, then smiled. ''Something like that.''

Lyons had heard enough. ''So,'' he said decisively, ''you want him dead. Fine.'' He gestured at Brognola. ''He wants him dead, too. That's enough for me. Just tell us where he is, and it's done. No problem.''

Julie shook her head. A look of pain passed over her face. ''Actually, there are a couple of problems.''

''What do you mean?''

"Well, it's not going to be that easy. In fact, it will be a hard kill."

"No sweat," rejoined Lyons.

"There's another problem."

"And that is?"

"We don't know where he is."

8

"So what do we expect to get out of this guy?"

Blancanales surveyed the landscape outside New York City as he spoke. A few miles ahead, off to the right, the sharp oblong shape of the Federal prison jutted above the rest of the buildings.

Gray clouds cloaked the sky; the eastern May sun made only a dull glow behind them. The width of the continent away, in Los Angeles and San Diego and points in between, people would be flocking to the beaches. Along the old boardwalk of Muscle Beach in Santa Monica, body builders would be pumping up in the open air, sweating with the effort of their training.

Not so New York. The weather stubbornly resisted the onset of springtime. Dirty gray was the order of the day. Lyons found himself wishing he were in L.A.

The Federal Metropolitan Correctional Center added to the effect. Compared to many of the state prisons throughout the country, the MCC looked modern and positively cheerful. But taken by itself, the structure made a foreboding monument to human evil.

From the driver's seat of the tan-and-brown van, Lyons shrugged. "Ask her," he replied, gesturing to Julie. His eyes scanned the freeway ahead for the off ramp for the prison.

Blancanales raised an inquiring eyebrow to the lady fed.

"Well," she began, "according to the file, he's the best lead we've got as to where Kadal might be."

"How so?"

"He's one of them."

"Who?" asked Lyons.

"Toruq. The man we're going to go see."

"No, I mean, who's he one of?" Lyons retorted impatiently.

Blancanales nudged his partner and winked. "Whom, Ironman. Remember the grammar lesson? Hal told us so; it's gotta be right."

Julie gave a little start, then smiled. "The Hizbullah, that's who."

"Who that be?" jived Gadgets from the rear of the van.

"It's called the Party of God. It's the most extremist of all the Muslims, at least in Lebanon."

"I thought that was the Shiites," observed Lyons from the driver's seat, recalling Brognola's comments during the briefing before Julie had arrived.

"What? Oh, I see," she responded. "It's this way. The Shiites are the most radical, all right, and the Hizbullah are the worst of the Shiites. They're the ones who want the Tri-Lateral Compact sabotaged."

Blancanales nodded his agreement. "The worst of the worst. The most extreme of the extreme," he commented. "That's going some."

Julie looked at him appraisingly. "You're right about that," she agreed. "You sound as if you know something about all this. How, uh..." She let the sentence trail, unfinished.

"You were going to ask, how did a trained killer and knuckle-dragger like me know about the Shiites and the Hizbullah?" Pol suggested with a grin.

She looked sufficiently embarrassed to show that was exactly what she'd been wondering. Blancanales let her stew for a few moments.

"I read the papers," he responded with a smile. "We all do, occasionally. Even Lyons, except he still has to move his lips. Sounds out the big words. We even read books occasionally. That is, when we're not ripping out throats, building bombs or practicing the latest in torture techniques. Right, guys?"

"Duh?" grunted Gadgets in his best Neanderthal voice.

"Kin-A," grunted Lyons in a voice that was even more Neanderthal than Gadgets's.

Julie looked at Blancanales. "What did he say?" she asked, gesturing at Lyons.

"Kin-A." Pol's face was perfect deadpan as he repeated the old military term.

"Oh."

Nobody spoke. Lyons looked straight ahead as he maneuvered the van off the expressway to get to the

MCC. Blancanales pretended to be gazing out the window. Finally, Julie broke the silence again, her voice sounding exasperated.

"All right, I'll bite, you guys. What is 'kin-a'? Some kind of Able Team code word?"

Blancanales stared at her, then bent his head forward and shut his eyes. With the thumb and first two fingers of his right hand, he stroked his forehead in a mock gesture of pain and disbelief. Gadgets, too, lowered his head, then turned and looked out the window, rubbing the back of his neck and emitting a muttered, "Sheesh!" Lyons, for his part, grimaced in feigned disgust, then cleared his throat and made a simulated spitting noise.

"Shee-itt. And she's going to be with us on this one?"

"Frightening," agreed Blancanales.

"Well, she is awfully young," pointed out Gadgets with a heavy sigh. Turning to Julie, he winked and put on his best professor's voice. "Kin-A, my dear girl, is a contraction of a time-honored military term. The *kin* sounds just like it would in *kinfolk*, and the *a* is long, like *able team*."

"What's it mean, though?"

He held up his hand imperiously. "Not yet, my dear. One step at a time. The pronunciation is important. Would you like to know how to pronounce it?"

"Of course," Julie responded good-naturedly.

"Good. These things are important. Now the proper pronunciation is with the emphasis on the *a*, like *delay*. Kin-A. Got it?"

She nodded, a resigned smile playing at the corners of her mouth. "Now may I ask what it means?"

Gadgets beamed. "I thought you'd never ask. It's a contraction, actually, of two words." He paused.

"And the two words?" she prompted.

"Fucking-a," he announced proudly.

Now it was Julie's turn to display the mock disgust.

"Fucking-a?" Her voice rose incredulously.

Gadgets nodded majestically, as did Lyons and Blancanales.

"And what, may I be so bold as to ask, does it mean?"

Gadgets shrugged. "Who knows? Something like *damned right*. Something like that."

"Gee. And to think I never knew," she murmured in good-humored sarcasm.

"Probably a product of public schools," muttered Lyons to the others, rolling his eyes. "Education system's a damned disgrace." Actually, he thought to himself, if she can handle this kind of kidding, this lady's going to be all right.

Assuming she *can* actually shoot, he added mentally.

"Anyway," Julie resumed, "you're right, of course. The Hizbullah are the most extreme of the extreme. In Lebanon, the Shiites are the radical underdogs of the Muslims. They were heavily involved in hijacking last year. In fact, there was actually a split among the Shiites because the Hizbullah always seem to oppose the release of any hostages. They want to kill them all.''

"To say nothing of thirty-two kids the other day," said Lyons bitterly. Julie nodded, but didn't respond.

"And this guy we're going to see is one of them?" inquired Blancanales.

She nodded. "The Bureau happened to find out— don't ask me how; probably an illegal wiretap—that he had a visitor from one of his fellow terrorists last week. They spoke in riddles, of course, but the belief is they were talking about Kadal and his mission."

"Not much to go on," observed Blancanales.

"What can I say? It's the best we've got."

"You're kidding," Lyons said flatly. "No other leads?"

She shook her head emphatically. "Nope. That's it. If we don't get something out of Toruq, we might as well fall back and just play bodyguard. Wait and see if we can stop it as it happens."

The Ironman shook his head bleakly. "The odds are a million to one against us."

Blancanales decided to turn the conversation back to a more productive line. "What's he in for?" he inquired.

"He was convicted of racketeering last year. Got sentenced to twenty-five years."

"What'd he do?"

"Bombs. Seems they proved he made one of the bombs used in a terrorist demonstration in New York three years ago."

"Anybody hurt?" asked Gadgets softly.

She nodded. "Six dead. Two of them were children."

"And we put him in prison for twenty-five years," said Lyons disgustedly. "Which probably means something like ten real years. *If* we're lucky. Why shouldn't we just kill him? Hell, kill him six times, if we could."

For a moment nobody spoke. Then Julie broke the silence. "Yeah, maybe. I didn't used to think that way. That was too uncivilized. But now I'm not so sure."

From the front seat, the ex-cop in Lyons spoke. "You see enough victims—I mean really see them, fresh, firsthand, bleeding and suffering and dying—you'll see what's right and what isn't about killing these bastards." His voice was hard and bitter.

"Maybe," Julie repeated. She paused and grimaced. "You know, I was talking to one of the agents on this guy's case. After they caught him, they advised him of his Constitutional rights, just like the book says. And do you know what he said?"

Lyons shook his head.

"He asked when they were going to torture him. And when he found out they weren't, he laughed and told them where they could stick their rights."

"And those six people are still dead, aren't they?" Visions of the skeleton in his dream flashed before him. Suddenly he turned to Julie, his eyes bright with speculation. "Could you do it?"

"Do what?"

"Kill him."

"Kadal?" she asked stupidly, stalling for time.

"Hell, yes, Kadal. Could you drop the hammer on him?"

"I think so. In self-defense, anyway."

"How about not in strictly speaking self-defense?"

"What do you mean?"

Lyons looked over at her for a moment. "Look. Say the guy's coming at you with a knife, or one of us, and we're down. You've got a gun. You could shoot him then, right?"

She nodded.

"Good. That's part of it, of course. But you know, don't you, that our directive—our orders—go beyond that."

She nodded again.

"To put it bluntly, we've been given a blank check to kill the bastard. Find him and kill him. Without notoriety, if possible. No headlines. No trial. Maybe no self-defense—just take him out if we can. Can you do it?"

After a long pause, she said despairingly, "I don't know. But I'm here, am I not?"

Lyons thought that over. It was a good answer, he decided, a better answer than if she had just said yes. "Have you ever killed anybody?"

She shook her head.

"Ever shot at anybody?"

"No."

Lyons turned away. His mind seethed with conflicting emotions. He liked this lady Fed, was strongly attracted to her, in fact. He would like to get to know her. He wanted to take her to dinner, to talk to her, to make her laugh. And, he admitted, to jump her bones.

Those feelings bothered him. For one thing, with a mission about to unfold, he didn't need the distraction. More than that, this promised to be a dangerous caper, and he didn't want her along, partly because she was an amateur and partly because of what else he felt.

To hell with it, he thought irritably. We'll probably get our asses shot off, anyway, and then it won't matter. Aloud, he responded to her last answer, his voice curt.

"Well, you may get your chance."

"Hey, Ironman, lighten up," said Blancanales quickly. "Save it for combat, you know?" He turned to Julie and continued, "Doesn't sound like this guy Toruq is likely to be too cooperative. What makes you think he's going to talk now? An acute attack of social conscience?"

Julie shook her head. "Actually, no. We're prepared to bargain with him a little, though."

"With what?" asked Blancanales. "Guys like this will do jail time standing on their heads. Hell, jail here is better than the way half his countrymen live at home."

"I know. But he has a brother who got caught on another terrorist caper. He's facing some heavy charges. I've got clearance to offer the brother leniency if this guy talks. Hopefully, he'll respond to that, even if he doesn't care about promises of leniency to himself."

None of the three men of Able Team voiced their shared but unspoken conviction. There was not a chance in hell Toruq would talk.

THE INTERVIEW ROOM was approximately ten feet by twelve. A Formica-topped table and three plastic chairs were the only items of furniture. Bright white light blazed from fluorescent bulbs. The place smelled of an astringent commercial cleanser.

A blue-uniformed guard led Toruq into the room. The terrorist moved with the characteristic prisoner's shuffle, made necessary by the security measures due to his extreme high-risk status. Chains encircled his waist. Manacles cuffed his hands to the waist chains on either side. Leg irons were fastened to his ankles, allowing only sixteen inches of movement for his feet.

The guard seated him in one of the plastic chairs, then left the room. Julie gazed at the prisoner, uncertain how to begin.

He was a dark young man who would have been handsome under other circumstances, she decided. Bottomless brown eyes dominated the broad planes of his face. A thin mustache ran along his upper lip. His hair was dark and curly and thick.

He sat without moving. Behind her, Julie was conscious of Lyons and Blancanales, leaning against the wall; Gadgets had elected to stay outside.

She began speaking. To herself, it seemed awkward at first, but then it got easier. She spoke slowly, her voice low-key and reasonable as she calmly made her points one after the other with straightforward logic.

Lyons admitted later he was impressed. She was a hell of a good lawyer.

Toruq was in prison, she said, and would remain there. Nothing she could do could change that. But it was different for his younger brother. He hadn't been sentenced; things could be done. His health was bad, and the prisons couldn't give him the medical assistance he needed.

Toruq could see that he got it. Release from prison, medical treatment at the best hospitals, protection, a new identity. It could be Toruq's gift, his legacy, the gift of life. He could show his love for his brother and thus serve Allah in a real and enduring way.

Throughout it all, Toruq never blinked. He sat in complete silence, motionless, his back straight and not touching the chair, giving no sign that he was even listening.

When she had finished, he didn't speak for several long moments. Finally he swallowed once, his Adam's apple bobbing convulsively in his lean throat.

"May I go now?" His voice was soft, almost respectful. It sounded surprisingly educated.

Julie felt a wave of dismay. "Toruq. What about your brother? What about Abdel?"

For the first time, he looked at her. "Abdel serves God, as do I. If that service calls upon us to die, we will do so."

"But for what?"

For the first time, he showed emotion. His eyes shone with the zealot's fervor. "It is my dream to die in the struggle against America and all who aid in the oppression of my people. To die in that way is to serve God. To do what you suggest is to betray God. This I will never do."

Julie started to speak again, but Toruq interrupted her.

"My people have driven bombs to the American Marine base in Beirut. We have driven the Israelis from the south part of Lebanon. The blood of our oppressors has been spilled and will be spilled again." He looked at her, his blazing eyes making a frightening contrast with his soft voice. "I may die. Abdel may die. But in the end our enemies will surely die."

Julie shook her head. The certainty of the man's will seemed insurmountable. She felt a sudden panic, as the hopelessness of their mission overwhelmed her. Would the bloodshed continue unabated, the slaughter of innocents perpetuated by the insanity of men such as this?

Suddenly Carl Lyons stepped forward. Hands on his knees, he bent down until his face was on a level with Toruq's.

"Toruq."

Lyons's voice was soft and deadly, his blue eyes diamond hard and colder than ice.

A power seemed to emanate from him, all the forces of life and death combined into one. Julie recoiled slightly from it. There was something familiar about it somehow, yet she couldn't put her finger on why.

Then he spoke again in the same low voice.

"Toruq, partner, let me tell you something. If I don't find that man in three days, and if he pulls off his little caper, *you* will surely die. You want to die in your cause, you want to serve God, then I'll see to it. Prisoner or not, chains or no chains, I promise I will kill you like a dog."

Lyons stood and walked toward the door. As he reached it, he turned and extended his hand, motioning for Julie to go ahead of him.

Again, the feeling of déjà vu struck Julie; this time it was Lyons's gesture that seemed familiar. What was it about the tableau that seemed so familiar?

For some reason she thought of Harper, and the head of Source One. But, try as she might, the connection eluded her. But for some reason she felt hopeless, bleak.

Jesus, she wondered, where is the little girl who went to Catholic schools and wanted to save the world? What has become of me?

She recalled her answer to Lyons's questions. *"I'm here, am I not?"*

But why are you here?

It's simple, she thought. I've made a partnership with Death.

Somehow it seemed she was a hell of a long way from home.

9

The dark, stocky man whose passport and other papers identified him as Kenneth Ibrahim felt the heat in his groin as he watched the young woman.

She wore only her undergarments, a bra and high-cut panties made of sheer blue nylon. She was beautiful, and she was stoned.

Chrome and glass furnishings dominated the suite. Shiny lamps threw circular pools of light in the otherwise dark room.

The girl stood in one of the circles, her bare feet sinking into the deep, jet-black carpeting. The ring of light cut across her at midthigh. Her legs made a startling human contrast to the stark modern decor. Above the light, her hips and the mysteries of her loins were concealed in the darkness. She swayed as she stood, as though in time to unheard music.

"Whore," Kadal said aloud.

The word excited him.

It meant he owned her, that he could do with her as he pleased. She was a nobody, a toy for his pleasure, a tool for him to gain sexual release. He was in command; she was his subject, his slave. She had to please him.

"Slut," he repeated.

She ignored him and continued her slow swaying.

He gave a mirthless laugh. This was his destiny, the service of his God in the tradition of the assassins, the Islamic terrorists and hashish eaters of nearly nine hundred years ago.

Kadal understood the legends of Hassan Ben Sabbah. The murder of the enemies of Islam became a duty, owed to God. No higher fulfillment existed than to serve in that fashion.

To kill was to serve God.

Death in the absolute sense did not exist to the assassins—to die in the service of God was to be born again, to serve again. Before killing, they consumed strong, bitter hashish to put them in the mood for killing.

Hashshashin, they were called. Hashish takers. Drugged killers who murdered as a religious duty, but who could not die themselves. The term was brought back to Europe by the Crusaders, who learned first-hand about the *hashshashin* in Syria. In time, the term had become *assassin*.

Kadal knew he was one of them. There were many in Hizbullah, men who would kill and die for the cause.

Up to now, Kadal's kills had been apolitical, purely mercenary. Pay the price, somebody dies. And he knew there was nobody better. If, somehow, a job proved to be impossible, he could walk away from it. But that hadn't happened yet.

This job was different.

This one was in the manner of the *hashshashin*, from whom he was descended. He was one of them, by blood and by trade. And the murder of the signers of the Tri-Lateral Compact—the Americans and the Israelis and even the traitors of Islam—was his calling.

He would not fail.

The clock was running, and he would soon be called upon to do his duty. But first, the pleasures of the flesh. . . .

The suite and the girl both belonged to an establishment referred to by the few who knew of its existence as Club 626.

Located in an elegant penthouse in the Upper East Side of Manhattan, Club 626 did not advertise. It did not recruit members or seek customers.

Personal referral by a member and invitation only were the standard operating procedures. The profile was low, the services tailored to the tastes of "discriminating" men and women. There was nothing that couldn't be arranged through Club 626.

Virtually nothing, anyway—no homicide or very young children; after all, the owners of 626 were not without principles.

Most of the clients were men, members of the financial or governmental power structure. The club could provide companions—male, female, or both—

of every ethnic and educational background and comfortable with every sexual persuasion.

For the right price, of course.

The young woman called herself Eva—tonight, anyway. She had a degree in English literature from a good private school. Her ties with 626 supported her in the life-style to which she had become accustomed.

Not particularly rewarding in some respects, she once described her profession, but relatively safe and highly lucrative.

Kadal, a.k.a. Kenneth Ibrahim, had the money and he had the references. That meant he also had the luxurious suite and the blond girl were his for the night. The only limitations were that he not significantly damage either one.

Or if he did, to pay for it.

He reached for a pouch made of soft, elegant leather. Unzipping it, he took out a mirror, a drug kit and a silver vial. He walked to a small table and sat in the black-and-chrome chair next to it.

The powder made a small mound on the mirror. It was a mixture of snowy white grains and tiny red crystals. The red ones tended to clump together and not be evenly dispersed in the rest of the powder. He took out a razor and chopped and stirred the little granular mixture. When he was done, the overall effect was a pale pink rather than red and white.

Skillfully the man used the blade to chivvy the powder into four long lines.

He took out a short silver tube and fitted it to his left nostril. With sudden animation, he vacuumed up one of the lines, stopping when the line disappeared, holding the inhalation. After several moments, he let out the air and fitted the tube to the other nostril. Another line vanished.

Kadal closed his eyes and rolled his head around on his neck. The rush of the drug hit him, a powerful combination of cocaine, amphetamine, and dicalcium aesthenase, called "di-cal" for short. One of the so-called "designer drugs," the di-cal was what gave the pink color to the final mixture.

The result was a double whammy—both a mild stimulant and a strong euphoric; combined with the coke and the speed, the effect was one of energy and euphoria combined.

"Come here, slut."

For a moment she didn't respond. Instead, she shut her eyes and continued to sway in the pool of light, languidly caressing the flat of her belly above the panties, taking sensory refuge in the effects of the cocaine and Quaaludes she had taken.

"Hey, slut," he repeated sharply. His voice enjoyed making the word, and he stretched it out in a guttural expression of disdain. "I said, come here."

Eyes still shut, she took a step toward him. It wasn't quick enough, for he suddenly leaped to his feet. He took two rapid strides and grabbed her by the hair at the back of her neck. Clutching his fist in the thick hair, he twisted her head back and levered her face upward.

"When I speak, you listen!"

She didn't respond. He gave a sharp jerk to his hand. "You hear me, whore?" he snarled through clenched teeth.

The girl opened her eyes and saw his contorted face. "Yes," she said softly.

"Yes, *sir*," he prompted.

"Yes, sir."

"Good. You want some?" He gestured at the table.

"Want some what?"

"Heaven, slut. A taste of heaven. You want some?"

She nodded, the movements restrained by the vice-like grip on her hair.

Suddenly Kadal swung his head from side to side in long, tense arcs. The muscles of his neck stood out as the combination of drugs jolted him in a monster second kick. He exhaled sharply, forcing the air out in a harsh grunt.

He felt all-powerful, a king, a god.

He put his mouth next to her ear and growled, "Beg me. Beg me for it."

The girl trembled. "Please, sir," she whispered, "may I have some?"

For a reply, he shoved her rudely at the table. She stumbled, then recovered her balance. Taking up the silver straw, she ingested the other two lines as easily as he had.

And waited.

She didn't have to wait long.

The drugs hit with a jarring rush. Eva shuddered as its effects, stacked on top of what was already in her system, surged over her and controlled her. Suddenly the room and its bright, expensive furnishings seemed to retreat, pulling away as if being sucked down a giant drain.

She had to hang on, to make it stop. She swung her head back and forth as he had done minutes before, trying to throw off the effects. Her own breathing sounded amplified, a roaring wind-tunnel effect through her nostrils. Then the room seemed to stabilize and she was in control again.

His voice came to her from somewhere a million miles away. At first she didn't understand, but then a phrase got through and made sense.

"Come here, slut."

Whatever else he had said, one thing was certain. She could not ignore that command. She had to respond to it, or he would hurt her.

She swung around. Her eyes scanned the pulsating room, then found him, sitting in a low black fabric armchair. His right hand was beckoning her, ordering her.

Eva made the trip on legs made of rubber and stood shakily next to his chair. She felt his hand on her leg, above her knee. It gripped her, then squeezed her, then hurt her, the powerful fingers digging into her soft flesh until she whimpered in pain. In an abstract corner of her mind, she knew there would be bruises the next day.

Another part reminded her that was what she was getting paid for.

He was speaking again, but she couldn't make out the words.

"What?" she managed, against the drugs. "Sir?" she added quickly.

Then she heard him and somehow understood the command. Her hands moved behind her back, up to the strap of her bra, fingers fumbling for the clasp. Then it was unfastened, and her breasts shifted forward slightly as the cups came free and the straps slid off her shoulders and down her arms. Her legs trembled uncontrollably from the steely grip of his fingers on her thigh.

He spoke again, his voice soft and brutal, taunting her, commanding her. She listened and obeyed, caressing her own breasts, pinching her nipples, arching her head back as she added her own pain to the pain he inflicted.

Then, suddenly, angrily, he was on his feet.

She felt herself lifted, plucked, thrown to the thick carpet. Heavy blows thudded into her head and body, partly dulled—but only partly—by the chemicals she had taken. She felt the tug on her panties and rolled and lifted her legs to try to help him. But it only seemed to make him more furious, and he picked her up and flung her against the thick glass coffee table.

She felt the flesh of her face yield and then break against the heavy glass surface. She saw the blood, and then the room began to retreat again.

She opened her eyes and saw him looming over her. A clenched fist was coming toward her face, and she tried to lift her arms to ward off the blow. But they felt leaden, as if tied to the floor. An explosion sounded in her head, and this time she let unconsciousness wash over her like a wave.

Her helplessness excited him.

The heat burned in his genitals, growing, tightening.

"Slut!" he shouted.

The woman did not move this time.

Kadal frowned, not understanding. The bitch was disobeying him, her god.

Suddenly something was wrong. Her pain wasn't enough any more. He felt the fire in his groin begin to subside. Panic swept over him, and he shut his eyes and clenched his teeth against it.

It was her fault.

A blind, furious rage exploded over him.

It dominated him, consumed him, possessed him. He was powerless before its fury, a red-hot anger that drove out any semblance of reason and left him filled with hatred.

Leaping to his feet, Kadal seized her. He lifted her off the ground and slammed her to the carpeted floor.

His genitals tightened as the warmth returned.

Then the lust was too much for him. He dropped to his knees beside her and began to peel down her underwear. He tore at his own clothing, freeing himself from his trousers. Then, dragging her panties off, he mounted her from behind.

Again and again, he rammed himself powerfully into her. Moments later, he realized she was dead, and the lust exploded into white-hot release.

At that moment, he knew his destiny.

He was the consummate assassin, and he could not be killed.

10

The telephone jangled on the motel room nightstand.

In the depths of sleep, Lyons at first had no idea what it was. By the time he recognized the ringing, he also knew he would have been dead had the sound been made by a foe rather than a phone.

He cursed his inaction and, as self-inflicted punishment for his slow reactions, made himself go through the survival drill even though he knew it was only the telephone.

He threw himself sideways off the bed, scrabbling for a weapon—a Kissinger-modified .45 auto—as he did so. He hit the floor and rolled, coming up at the ready, gun in hand and feeling foolish.

"Good morning, Ironman."

Blancanales grinned as he spoke to his partner. Jungle-trained to the core, the Politician always slept lightly. He was already answering the phone even as Lyons launched his body off the bed.

"Able here," he said into the receiver. As he listened for the reply, he shot a perplexed look at Lyons. His partner was crouched on the floor in his skivvies, hair sticking up in all directions, gun in hand.

"Stand by for Stony Man," said the voice on the other end.

As he waited, Blancanales covered the mouthpiece with his free hand. "That was real cute, Ironman. Spectacular, even."

Lyons merely grunted, rubbing his knee where it had banged against the wrought-iron base of the fake wood-grain Formica motel room table. In the third bed, Gadgets Schwarz, who had known it was the telephone and hadn't bothered to react, rolled over with a sleep-drenched groan.

"Pretty slow, of course," continued the Politician.

"Up yours," Lyons muttered.

"Still, I don't suppose they could have gone through more than a clip or two before you reacted, so maybe it's okay, after all."

Red-faced, Lyons shook his head and got stiffly to his feet. He checked to make sure the .45 was still locked—he always carried it "cocked and locked"—and set it on the table.

Blancanales delivered the final barb. "At least it's probably faster than our lady Fed can do it. Maybe it's even fast enough to take Kadal."

"What the hell," Lyons grumbled. "At this rate, we'll probably never find the scum, anyway, so it won't matter."

Blancanales shrugged. "Don't be too sure, amigo. I have the feeling something is about to happen."

A cheerful, familiar voice barked in his ear from the telephone. "Brognola here."

"Yeah, Chief."

"Roll your asses out of bed and get ready to move," the Stony Man Operations Director continued. Blancanales winced at the booming voice and held the receiver away from his head. From his position several feet away, Lyons could hear Brognola's words directly. "We may be about to get our big break."

Pol looked at Lyons and grinned. Aloud, he spoke into the telephone. "Where are we going?"

"You're going to mingle with the high rollers for a while. Or at least, you are going to the place where some of them hang out."

"Where's that?"

"Manhattan. Upper East Side. A place called the 626 Club."

The Politician grinned, forgetting that Brognola couldn't see it over the telephone. "Sounds ritzy. I'll try to keep Lyons on a leash. We gonna see any celebrities?"

Brognola's laugh boomed over the line. "Doubtful. The place is basically a whorehouse, but a high-class one. It seems pretty likely that the customers, celebrities or not, will be adios'd by the time you get there, or at least trying to keep real low-pro."

Lyons nudged his partner. "Ask him if they give out free samples."

Blancanales rolled his eyes, but declined the invitation. "Just what are we supposed to find there?"

"Or maybe even a secret agent discount," Lyons prompted in a low voice.

"What's Lyons quacking about?" boomed Brognola.

"Nothing, Chief," said Blancanales quickly. "Just ignore him. Just what are we supposed to be doing at Madam Wong's, or whatever it is?"

Over the phone, they could hear Brognola take a deep breath and let it out slowly. "With any luck, you're going to find Kadal was just there. If that's so, it'll put you only a couple of hours behind him."

The two men of Able Team looked at each other. This could be it, all right. Then Blancanales spoke up.

"What happened, anyway?"

Brognola chuckled, but it sounded more depressed than humorous. "As I said, it's a whorehouse. Your basic bordello. Seems Kadal may have been there for a little R and R earlier this evening, or last night, technically."

"And?" prodded Blancanales.

"It looks like he got carried away and murdered one of the girls."

"How?"

"Beat her to death."

Blancanales let out a soft whistle. Behind him, Lyons chimed in. This time there was no horseplay.

"Ask him if the cops are there."

"Yep," boomed Brognola's voice, even before Blancanales repeated the question. "They're about to call it a wrap, but they'll stand by until you get there. They've been briefed to give you whatever cooperation you need. In fact, they're sending a car over now.''

"Good. We'll follow them in the van. They can show us how to get around this goddamned city.''

"Why not just ride with them?''

Blancanales shook his head. "Uh-uh. This way, we'll have everything we need if the shooting starts. That's the idea, isn't it?''

Lyons was already stepping into his Levi's. He grabbed Pol's trousers and tossed them to him. The Politician bent his head to one side, clamping the receiver against his shoulder to free his hands so he, too, could begin getting dressed. Across the room, Gadgets was up and moving.

"Anything else we should know?'' the Politician inquired.

Behind him, Lyons buckled his belt and knocked on the door that joined their room with the one occupied by Julie.

"Let's roll it!'' he called cheerfully. "Reveille! Call to arms!''

As he spoke, Lyons allowed himself to engage in the brief but pleasant speculation as to what she was probably wearing at that moment.

And how she looked wearing it.

As well as how she probably looked changing from whatever she had been wearing to whatever she would be wearing.

And, as long as he was on the subject, how she would look in his arms. Pretty good, he'd be willing to bet.

And—to get down to business—whether they would ever catch up with that bastard Kadal, and what would be the outcome if they did. How many would die, and who they would be.

"Nothing startling," came Brognola's voice in response to the Politician's question. "Everything's still on track for the little signing party day after tomorrow."

"It's still a go?"

"So far. It's not cast in concrete, of course, but it looks as if it'll go through. Unless..."

They all knew the sentence wasn't complete. It was a hell of a big "unless" that was attached to the end of it—unless we don't somehow stop Kadal.

Whether the bastard succeeded in killing everybody, or anybody, was no longer the only question. Even the fact of a close call could still undermine the shaky confidence underlying the treaty and cause it to abort.

Brognola spoke again. "The President has asked that I convey his sincerest wishes for success in your mission."

"Yes, Chief."

Blancanales shook his head, more to himself than to Lyons or Gadgets. Normally, Brognola knew what his men were going through and didn't add to the stresses by recitals of how much depended on it. Obviously, the pressure was building.

" 'Whatever it takes,' was how he put it, I believe."

"Yes, Chief." There wasn't anything else to say.

"Yeah. I know you know. Good luck. Stony Man out."

"Able out."

DETECTIVE-SERGEANT CHUCK CURTIS was about six and a half feet tall. He looked as if he should have been a deputy sheriff in some western state rather than the supervisor of Team Twelve of a big-city homicide bureau. He wore cowboy boots beneath a conservative business suit, assuming conservative is a term that can be applied to a size 54 long. The overall effect was a Texas Ranger goes to Wall Street.

He was also, Lyons realized immediately, one very sharp cop beneath the low, slow voice and sleepy eyes.

Curtis ordered the rest of his men from the area when Able Team arrived.

As he sized up the group he remembered that his orders had been clear: full cooperation and no questions. He hadn't been told with whom he was cooperating, other than that it was "some bunch of goddamned federal strike force assholes, I guess."

But the call—and that description—had come from the police commissioner himself. Whoever these guys were, he decided, they had some juice. If that's what the commissioner wants, that's what the commissioner gets.

Still, as he looked at Able Team now, it didn't seem as irritating as he had thought it would be.

He had expected a group of soft-handed Ivy League Feds with impressive credentials and shiny, unused guns in shoulder holsters; guys who could investigate the hell out of an investment fraud but who had never had to walk in on a bar fight with nothing but your uniform and your guts as backup.

Whatever he had expected, it was wrong. These guys weren't that way.

The blond man was obviously a street cop, or had been. To Curtis, it was written all over him. The Latino guy had a lot of specialized military about him; SWAT, maybe. The older man with the gray hair was harder to call, but there was a definite ruggedness about him. It bespoke a lot of practice at taking care of himself.

And then there was the woman.

Curtis wasn't sure about her, either. Almost reflexively, he had decided "token female." But as he watched her, that didn't fit. She was younger than the rest, and she undoubtedly didn't have the combat experience of the others. But she exhibited a quiet competence, a sort of indefinable toughness, which explained her presence better than token did.

She had a look that suggested when the chips were down, she would come through.

Damned few broads had that quality. This was one of them.

Lyons scanned the suite's ultramodern furnishings with a practiced eye. "Who made the report?"

Curtis shook his head ruefully. "That's kind of delicate. The woman who runs the place, uh, knows one of the captains on the department. She called him, and he told her how to call in the report. Leaving his name out of it, of course."

Lyons grinned. "Which she didn't do, obviously."

The big detective returned the grin. "She thought she could get away with just telling me the truth."

"And?"

"I pointed out a couple of inconsistencies in her statement, and she finally gave me the whole truth. Or at least what is the present version of the whole truth."

"He's a friend of hers?"

"Who?"

"The captain."

Curtis nodded. "Yeah. Either that or a customer. Come to think of it, probably can't be one without the other."

"This place have a lot of friends like that? Influential friends?"

"Probably. Enough, anyway. What can I say?" The New York's cop's voice sounded disgusted.

Lyons shrugged. "Fact of life in the big city. What do you have on the suspect?"

Curtis ran it down for him.

The girl was a prostitute, employed by the club. Apparently she had been beaten to death—final diagnosis would have to come from the pathologist after the autopsy, but her body showed numerous bruises consistent with having been kicked. Extensive damage was present on her face. Deep bruises just above one knee. She'd had intercourse shortly before death.

Lyons wrinkled his brow. "Wouldn't it take an autopsy to make that determination?"

Curtis shook his head. "In this case, it was obvious. It's even possible he killed her right afterward."

Lyons remembered his hunch about Kadal from the photograph. "Or even right before," he murmured.

"What's that? I didn't hear you," said Curtis quickly.

"Nothing. Anything else?"

Curtis took out a small notebook and consulted it. A drug kit—mirror, razor and silver straw—found. Traces of powder, white and red.

"Red?" asked Lyons. "A powder?"

Curtis nodded.

"What the hell kind of drug would that be?"

"We're having the lab analyze it. My guess is it is either some kind of 'cut'—in which case, it isn't really a drug itself—or some one of the newfangled 'designer drugs.' Hell, with all the chemists these dopers have working for them, it could be God knows what variation of a dozen drugs. It's gotten so bad, the law can't keep up with listing the illegal ones. Statute comes out with more of them on the list, and a month later they've found new ones."

Lyons thought that over. Then he remembered that he wasn't really concerned with all the law enforcement aspects of the case. What he needed was to know if Kadal had done it. And, if they were really lucky, where he might be.

It was a delicate question to broach, however.

As a former cop himself, Lyons knew that more than one case had been blown by too many details being released too early in the investigation. That meant that cops, who are by nature a secretive and suspicious lot, invariably guarded their evidence carefully, even jealously.

Lyons guessed that Curtis was probably under orders to assist them. In any event, the big detective had concealed any animosities at discussing the case up to this point. Still, Lyons kept his voice as casual as possible, almost indifferent, as he brought up the subject.

"Any suspects?"

Curtis nodded. "That's why you're here, isn't it?" When Lyons didn't respond, he went on. "Guy named Kenneth Ibrahim. At least that's the name he was using."

"How do you know that?"

"Official influence goes only so far. Even here in New York. This is a murder, and a bad one in some ways. We, uh...*counseled* with the proprietors of this establishment, and they opened up pretty good as to what they knew about this customer."

Lyons grinned.

Somehow he bet that Curtis was pretty effective at "counseling" reluctant witnesses, in a method that was perfectly proper and did not involve physical persuasion. And was probably more effective than those methods that did. "What did they tell you?"

"Physical description, of course. Who referred him. Where he was staying. That sort of thing."

"So tell me."

The description fitted Kadal perfectly.

"Where's he staying?" Lyons asked excitedly. This was it, he thought, the big break.

Curtis shook his head. "No help there. Phony address."

Lyons's heart sank. Of course it would be a fake address, he thought bitterly. It couldn't be that easy.

"But we got something else," said Curtis.

"What?"

"Vehicle description. Valet remembered his car. Kid wants to be a cop. Taking home-study courses in police science. Goes around practicing observing things."

"And he remembered Kadal, uh, the suspect?"

Curtis looked curiously at Lyons, but did not press him on the slip. "Well, he got the info on the car. Make, year, model, plate. We ran it, and it came back to a leasing company."

"And?"

"And we got the leasing people out of bed. They checked the records, and got an address where it was delivered."

Lyons was beside himself with excitement. "When?" he demanded.

"Day before yesterday."

The Ironman turned to his companions. "That fits! That's when he would have gotten here from L.A.! This could be it."

Blancanales spoke up. "What are you doing with the information?"

For the first time, Curtis looked a little unhappy. "Right now, we're sitting on it," he said shortly. "Freeze on it until you guys got here."

"There's something else I was wondering," continued the Politician. "How'd you get flagged to bring us in on it, anyway?"

"You guys—whoever the hell you are—or some other Fed, must have had a BOL on the suspect name, or the name he was using. We had no sooner run it on the computers than the commissioner got a call from some big fish in D.C. telling him to sit tight."

Blancanales looked puzzled. "What's a BOL?"

Lyons answered. "'Be on the lookout.' It's like red-flagging it. They can put a code into the computers so that if anybody runs the name, somebody gets notified."

Curtis nodded his agreement. "I don't know for sure, of course, but that must be what happened. Because we sure as hell got called as soon as we ran that name."

He gave them the address. It was a posh penthouse in what was definitely the high-rent district of Manhattan.

Lyons turned to the others. "Let's go," he snapped tersely. Then he hesitated and turned back to Curtis. "Thanks," he said awkwardly.

The big detective's face was impassive, but his voice was cool. "No sweat."

Lyons shook his head. "Yeah, it is. I used to be a cop. I know what it's like. You get dragged out of bed in the middle of the night, then work your ass off on some dreary goddamned case. Then maybe you make it, get a good break and some prima donnas from some secret squirrel outfit swoop down and take over. And you go along with it because 'orders is orders.'"

Curtis shrugged. "Goes with the territory."

"Yeah, maybe. But I want you to know that I've been there. If we pull this off, it'll be partly because of the good work you guys did."

A faint smile pulled at the corners of the homicide detective's mouth. "I know you probably won't tell me, but just what *are* you trying to pull off, anyway?"

"Urban pest control."

"What do you mean?"

The Ironman avoided the question. "When I was a cop," he said slowly, "we had several ways to end an investigation."

"Yeah. So?"

"Methods like, 'Case closed, no leads.' 'Case closed, suspect i.d.'ed, warrant sought.' 'Case closed by arrest.' Or, sometimes, a fourth category, 'Case closed, suspect deceased.' You have something similar?"

"Basically, yeah."

Lyons smiled, It was a wintry smile, devoid of warmth or humor. "What I'm trying to pull off is to make this case fall in the fourth category. You get my drift?"

Detective Sergeant Curtis looked at them for a long moment. Then, slowly, a grin spread over his broad, cowboy features.

"Gotcha," he said finally.

"Thanks again for the help." Lyons moved to the door where the others were already waiting.

"Hey, Lyons?" Curtis's voice called him back.

"Yeah?"

"When it's all over, give me a call."

"Sure."

"Just to let me know how to mark the file, okay?"

Lyons grinned and nodded. "Gotcha."

11

Detective Sergeant Curtis had not been wrong when he said that the address was definitely in the high-rent district.

The Able Team van rolled through the darkened streets, following the directions the homicide detective had given. Lyons had the wheel, and Blancanales called out the turns from the shotgun seat. Gadgets, meanwhile, began to get out their gear.

"Carl," Julie began from the back of the van, behind Pol's seat.

"Yeah?"

"Did you know that detective? Curtis?"

"No."

She fell silent. Then she spoke again, leaning forward. Lyons could see her face in the soft glow of the dashboard lights. It was dark and intense and forceful. And beautiful.

"Why did you tell him what we were going to do?"

"What do you mean?"

"That business about the fourth category. 'Case closed, suspect deceased.' I can't believe you did that."

"Why not?"

"Well, you might as well have just told him we're going to assassinate the guy."

Lyons thought that over as he drove. "Look," he finally replied, "I know what you're saying. On the surface, it does look like a breach of security."

"You got that right," she rejoined with considerable emphasis.

"But it was just one of those calls you make. I felt like I could trust the guy. To some extent, he was entitled to know. But the main reason I went ahead and said that was because it just might help us out."

"I can't wait to hear how you figured that."

Lyons grinned at her in the darkness. "I used to be a cop, remember? Apart from knowing how it feels to have somebody else take over your case, I also know he'll be getting pressure from above to close the file by making an arrest."

"So? All we have to do is get somebody to tell them not to, that it's a federal case," Julie said.

Typical federal approach, thought Lyons. He kept the thought to himself.

Aloud, he said, "Fine. But that only works so far. A lot of cops resent that. They'll bitch about it, tell half their buddies how the Feds stole the case. A few might even try to go around us and do it, anyway." He paused.

"Go on," Julie said.

"This way, we've got an ally. Curtis looks like he would be respected in the department. I'm betting he'll keep his guys quiet, as much as he can. And if some captain starts grousing about the Feds, maybe talking about going to the papers, I have the hunch that Curtis will be able to back our play to some extent. Smooth the ruffled feathers.''

"Seems like an 'if' followed by a 'maybe,' " Julie observed at last, shaking her head. "I hope you know what you're doing."

Lyons shrugged. "I don't *know* what I'm doing. Like I said, I'm betting that's how it will come out."

Blancanales ended the debate with an urgent, "There it is!"

The Towers looked as if it had been folded out of paper, like some model for an architect's rendering of a futuristic skyscraper. It was a tall rectangle with lots of right-angle creases that ran vertically up the building. It looked about twenty stories high.

A concrete ramp resembling a channel led down below the street. At both the top and the bottom of the ramp, heavy iron security gates spanned the opening. There were TV monitors trained on the driveway at both gates.

Lyons cruised slowly by until he found a place to park. He shut off the engine and crawled into the rear of the van.

"Let's suit up." His voice was curt, all business.

Suit up they did. Lightweight Kevlar body armor went on over their T-shirts. Over that, ordinary long-sleeved street shirts.

In one sense, the shirts were ordinary. In another they were anything but. The colors were dark blue and dark green, blended together in a modern-appearing pattern. Worn above dark blue or black Levi's, the overall effect was of dark-colored, mod-style casual dress.

The shirts had been the brainchild of Cowboy Kissinger, Stony Man's new weapons expert.

The effectiveness of any camouflage depended on several factors, including the lighting and the background, Kissinger had explained. No pattern works in every setting.

The Cowboy's theory was that the blending of dark blue and dark green made a fairly effective camouflage at night, especially for inner city work, where vegetation did not supply the predominant backdrop. Yet in the daylight, there was a good chance the clothing would pass for ordinary casual dress, thus not identifying the wearer as a SWAT officer.

"Why not just issue signal orange fatigues with SWAT written all over them?" the Cowboy had once remarked sarcastically, when asked to comment on the use of traditional camouflage fatigues by urban SWAT officers.

Over the shirts went nylon shoulder-holster rigs, each holding a Kissinger-tuned .45 Government model.

Kissinger-tuned meant the .45s were the best in the world. Balanced, honed, a different slide-spring—these guns were to the Gold Cup, which was Colt's "custom" model of the .45 Government model, what the Gold Cup was to the basic workhorse item.

Balancing the .45 under the other arm, the shoulder rigs held four clips of Silver-tip. Each round was 185 grains of specially designed, partially jacketed projectile. Each could be counted on to deliver some 400 foot-pounds of energy to the target.

"Definitely discouraging," as Kissinger put it. "Not the end of the rainbow as far as combat handguns are concerned, but the best for now."

"What *is* the end of the rainbow?" Blancanales had inquired.

"I'm working on it," had been the cryptic reply.

Over the shirts and shoulder holsters went lightweight casual jackets. The firearms were completely concealed; to the casual observer, there were three men dressed in street clothes.

But the .45s were strictly secondary weapons. Backup. Gadgets opened another metal case and began passing out the mainstay firearms.

Once again, it was a case of Kissinger improving on nature, or on the factory item, in this case. The streetlight reflected off the deadly black molecular coating finish on the Stony Man version of the 9 mm Uzi Assault Pistol.

A stubby-looking machine pistol, the Uzi had a T-shaped, right-angle appearance. This was due to the thick pistol grip that jutted down at ninety degrees from nearly the center of the weapon. Kissinger had modified the pistol so it could be fired full-auto, with a selector switch mounted on the side of the receiver. He had shortened the trigger pull and made it more crisp, and had honed and balanced the entire weapon in the same manner he had with the .45s.

The sporting model of the Uzi Pistol—semiautomatic only—came with a 20-round magazine. Kissinger had opted for a specially made 30-round model. It projected somewhat below the pistol grip, but Able Team believed the increase in firepower was worth the loss of symmetry.

It was a deadly, efficient weapon, even if somewhat blunt and ugly by the standards applied to conventional handguns.

Wordlessly, Gadgets passed one to each of them.

To Julie, the handing out of the weapons had a sort of ritual overtone. Though nobody spoke, the young agent had the definite feeling she was being tested, or at least closely observed, by the others. Accordingly, she accepted the pistol casually, cleared and checked it expertly and held out her hand.

"Clip?"

Gadgets handed one to her. She inserted it and clapped it home into the grip, released the bolt and made sure the safety was on.

"Got any spare clips?"

Behind her, Lyons looked at Blancanales and winked. Gadgets found two more clips and handed them to her, then passed them to each of the others. Finally, Lyons had to speak out.

"Have you, uh, ever used one of those before?"

"Who? Me?" she deadpanned.

"No, the lady next to you," he said, grinning. "Of course you. Who else?"

She shook her head. "Never even held one before. I just cleared it and loaded it by accident."

"Yeah, right." Lyons, who had been already turning away, jerked back and looked at her closely. When he saw her look, he realized he had been taken in.

"Beginner's luck," she went on.

"Okay, okay," he said ruefully. "So you've fired one before. Can you hit anything?"

Her gaze was cool, challenging. "Well enough," she reminded him. "I can handle it."

Their eyes met for an instant. He started to make an off-color quip, but thought better of it.

Instead, he just nodded. "I hope so" was his only reply.

Gadgets next took out a black nylon kidney pack. It resembled an oversize belt with nylon pouches attached in the back. He buckled it on, then put on a loose-fitting hip-length jacket over it. The belt was concealed. When he was finished putting his own in place, Gadgets brought out two more.

He examined one carefully by the light of a flashlight, then nodded and handed it to Lyons. He gave the other to Blancanales.

Julie watched this in silence.

This can't be real, she thought. Here it is the middle of the night—a couple of hours before dawn, anyway. I'm with three men who, regardless of the fact they seem like pretty nice guys, are essentially paid killers for the U.S. government. We're parked on an ordinary street in the middle of one of the biggest cities in the world, and we're all getting suited up for a firefight.

Dressed to kill, she thought, with a wry, inward smile at her own bad joke. And to think that her mother used to worry she might be mugged if she stayed out past midnight.

She wrenched her mind back to the business at hand. "Have you given any thought to how you are going to get past the security?"

Lyons nodded.

"How?"

"You."

"Me?"

"Yeah. You're going to get us in."

"How?"

"Sure. Show 'em your badge and talk FBI to them. Everybody cooperates with the FBI. It'd be un-American not to."

She thought that over. "Don't we need a warrant?"

Lyons nodded. "Probably."

"You got one?"

"Why ask a question you already know the answer to?"

"We going to get one?"

"Nope."

"I see. Just asking, that's all."

Lyons looked at her. "Look. You guys tried it legally, and your mission fell on its own sword. My orders don't say anything about any warrants. If you're worried you might have to testify against us someday, say so now, and bail out. You can't testify to what you don't know about."

She returned his look, her eyes bottomless brown pools. "I'm not worried about that."

"Good."

Lyons winked at her. "The way I see it is like this. Does a warrant make him any less bulletproof? Does it make us any more bulletproof?"

She didn't respond.

"Then I guess we don't need one, do we?"

THE ELEVATOR DOORS OPENED with a quiet whisper. Deep brown carpeting covered the floor ahead of them. The walls were covered with a muted, expensive wallpaper. A floor-to-ceiling mirror covered the wall opposite the elevator.

Julie gazed at their images in the mirror. Something about seeing their reflections—herself and the three men, one of them being the rugged blond man with the tired eyes—seemed familiar. Then, suddenly, she had it.

It was what had been lurking in the recesses of her mind, the thing she had been groping for earlier.

The safe house. Harper. The head of the poor woman they called Source One. Specifically, it was the collage of images, the vision, for want of a better word, that she had seen as she blacked out.

The proud animal with the power of death.

It was Lyons.

The other two had to be Blancanales and Gadgets.

These were the images she had seen, or imagined, back in the safe house, what seemed a lifetime ago but was actually only a couple of days.

She remembered something else from the vision. There would be much blood. Many would die before this was over. And she was a part of it. She'd made a partnership with Death.

Somehow it seemed like a hell of a long way from home.

"You got the key?" Lyons's voice broke into her thoughts.

Wordlessly, Julie held it out to Lyons. It had been given to them by the doorman who was, as Lyons predicted, impressed by Julie's FBI and Department of Justice credentials.

Only two suites opened off the foyer, Kadal's and one other. The team had moved quickly to the right door.

They gathered by the door.

It was painted an elegant off-white. The doorknob and lock were of expensive brushed brass. A few feet to the right stood a shiny metal container with a graceful arrangement of dried plants. Their pungent, spicy odor lingered in the hushed air.

Lyons flattened himself against the wall and raised the Uzi. He held it muzzle up to his side near his head as he prepared himself for the entry.

The weapon's surface had been Parkerized, then coated with a black molecular finish. Kissinger had added custom Pachmyer-style grips. Deeply checkered, the grips were made of rubber, not hard and not soft, exactly. *Tacky* was a good word for the way it felt.

Lyons had used similar grips, the Pachmyers, in his cop days on his service revolver, generally either a Colt Python or a Smith & Wesson Model 19 in .357 Magnum caliber. They made the weapon easier to hold on to. That meant it didn't shift in his hand from the recoil of the shots, the way it had a tendency to do with wood grips. Kissinger had adapted the concept to the Uzi, which tended to buck considerably when the bolt slammed forward, especially when fired in auto-burn.

Lyons recalled how some cops were concerned that the flat black of the Pachmyers didn't look as stylish as the shiny walnut grips that came from the factory. On the other hand, in his book, they gave a look of deadly efficiency to the weapon.

That look had fitted the Ironman then, and it fitted him now.

As he held the pistol up by his shoulder, Lyons extended and then flexed his fingers around the thick grip, settling the weapon into his fist. As he put his trigger finger into place and flicked the weapon to auto-burn, his gaze fell on his hand and the blunt, brutish weapon in it. Beyond them he saw the muted beauty of the wallpaper and the ivory door. Even beyond that, fuzzy because he was focused on the pistol, were the graceful curves of the dried plant display.

The Uzi was purely functional. The function was to knock down, to inflict damage, to rupture and tear flesh.

Ultimately, to kill.

The tasteful furnishings that formed the backdrop were purely aesthetic. Their function to please the eye, to depict beauty, to provide pleasure.

The contrast between the two gave him a strange disorientation, a surreal feeling of images out of context. It was a jolting, unpleasant juxtaposition—an ugly tool like a blacksmith's hammer in a china dish.

Or violent death amid peaceful beauty. Shattered flesh on satin sheets.

He pushed the thought from his mind. With one continuous motion, he took the key in his left hand, inserted it, turned the lock and then the knob and kicked the door inward.

Lyons followed the door as it swung open.

He let the momentum of his kick carry him inside, then he dived forward in a long, slanting dive inside the room. Behind him, Blancanales also rushed in, going in the opposite direction, while Gadgets knelt at the door frame, ready to give covering fire.

The weak rays of night-lights illuminated the interior of the penthouse. Before them lay a spacious sitting room. To the right was an elegant bar of polished walnut and black leather, with rows of glassware and bottles in front of a smoked-glass mirror. Next to the bar, a hallway led off to the right. Straight ahead on the far side of the sitting room lay an elegant kitchen, all tile and oak and shiny appliances.

For two or three heart-stopping seconds, there was no response to the sound of Able Team's entry. Lyons and Blancanales took advantage of the inaction to scrabble ahead and to each side, going for cover and putting as much distance as possible between each other.

Suddenly there was a rustle of movement in the semidarkness, then someone shouted in a foreign tongue, but the message was clear.

A warning.

From her position outside the door, Julie heard the yell and the answering gunfire. The battle has begun, she thought. The killing has started.

Where, how, would it end?

The shape of a man loomed up from a sofa in the room ahead of them. There was no mistaking his purpose. As he shouted, the sentry started to raise his weapon—a submachine gun, with the stamped-metal look of one of the imitations of the Uzi, thought Lyons—Lyons swung his machine pistol to bear.

He didn't make it in time. From the doorway, Gadgets fired first, a sharp, short burst that took the gunner full on in the chest. A coarse spray of blood spattered the drapes and bookcase beyond the couch.

12

As the Ironman swung his own weapon to bear on the hardman, he shouted a warning to his companions.

"Look out!"

Adrenaline surged through him. This was it, he thought exultantly. The vacation was over. The waiting was behind him, the battle about to be joined. He felt quick and alert and dangerous, ready to do what had to be done for a good cause.

Ready to kill.

Not afraid to die, if it came to that. But, like a running back plunging toward the goal, he wasn't going to be knocked off his feet easily.

To hell with the skeleton in the shroud. Lyons felt the pent-up energy of frustration and rage against these scum-suckers who murdered children in the fiery blasts of terrorist-made bombs. It surged to the surface and drove him into battle.

Shooting by instinct, he pressed the trigger as the Uzi lined up with the sentry.

Even as he fired, Lyons knew he was too late.

From his crouched position in the doorway, Gadgets fired a neat, concise burst. The 9 mm slugs struck home in the man's chest at some twelve hundred feet per second. Lyons's own volley, a split second later, hit already dying or dead flesh.

The impact drove the killer backward, as though jerked from behind by an invisible wire.

A spray of bright crimson erupted as the 9 mm fusillade struck home. It spattered the expensive drapes and wallpaper, and ran down the walls in long red rivulets.

Lyons wasted no time as he shouted, "Let's go!"

He sprinted into the sitting room, hurling a low chair without breaking stride. He ran past the dead man and checked the kitchen. Satisfied there was nothing in that direction, he looked back over to the right, to the hallway by the bar.

"That way!" he snapped at Blancanales. But even as he spoke, Lyons caught sight of the enemy.

A broad-shouldered man with thick dark hair and mustache loomed in front of him. He, too, held an automatic weapon, but Lyons was way ahead of him.

The Ironman clamped his hand on the Uzi and fired. He was a good second or two ahead of his adversary on getting the firepower into action. Autoburn all the way, he thought. The Uzi spat two rounds...

And jammed.

"Shit!" The oath exploded from Lyons's throat.

Both slugs had been knock-down shots, dead center in the trunk of the body, the center of mass. But the man didn't go down.

Instead, he took the two hits almost in stride. He was a strong dude, part of Lyons's mind realized with the respect one soldier can have for another, even an enemy. The only visible sign of the hits was a single grunt that was forced from his body a second after the hits. Then, after only a moment's hesitation, the man continued to bring up his own weapon.

Lyons slammed the heel of his hand against the slide on the Uzi.

Nothing.

"Shit!" he yelled again, and threw the weapon aside. With the same motion, he reached for the .45 in his shoulder holster.

Though both men moved at lightning speed, to Lyons it seemed as if every second was divided into a hundred frames, and that he could see each one. Even as he went for the other gun, the Ironman knew that luck, skill and timing had to all be with him if he was to live.

They were, by one or two frames. Two-hundredths of a second, maybe.

The .45 roared twice. It made a heavier, more authoritative boom than the staccato chatter of the Uzi.

Two for two. Both head shots. The stocky soldier went down in a boneless heap.

Lyons didn't take the time to reflect on the kill. "That way!" he snapped again to Blancanales, pointing to the hallway by the bar, off to the right.

The Vietnam Special Forces veteran didn't have to be told. He had rolled until he was covering the hallway the instant he had seen and heard the firepower directed at the sentry.

Even as Lyons shouted the order, a door opened down the hallway. Three men burst out. Each carried a machine gun like the one the sentry had carried. None of them bumped into any of the others—they looked as if considerable practice had gone into the maneuver.

The impromptu fire team swung their weapons up at Lyons.

"Die, you fuckers!" The words tore from the Ironman's throat in a long, agonized shout. He crouched and swung the .45 to bear on the targets, firing as fast as he could.

One of the terrorists yelled something in reply. It was cut short in midsentence as three Able Team weapons opened fire. Vivid orange streaks slashed the semidarkness, accompanied by the thunderous hammering of the blasts.

The hail of bullets cut two of the men down instantly. The third threw himself to one side, back flat against the wall of the hallway. Bracing his machine gun on his hip, he unleashed a volley back toward the sitting room.

Blancanales and Lyons dived for cover.

Pol made a lateral dive that put him against a wall, out of the line of fire. He hit, rolled and started to get into position to fire back in case the shooter advanced, or, as the alternative, to advance himself.

Lyons had farther to go for cover. He took a quick, short step and then threw himself toward safety.

He wasn't fast enough.

Something smacked into his head on the right side, just above his ear. It made a sudden, deadening thump as it struck. The impact snapped his head back.

Lyons felt his knees weaken and buckle. The dim room suddenly got darker, then started to swim before his eyes. The Ironman staggered and fell slowly forward, his momentum gone. He clawed to his hands and knees, crawling for cover. Then they, too, gave out, and he pitched forward on the expensive carpet, staining its muted elegance with his life's blood.

"I'm hit!" he tried to shout.

The room swirled and seemed to recede. All he could make out were shapes. As if to compensate, his other senses suddenly became alive, hypersensitive, many times more powerful than normal.

Lyons felt the soft rug beneath him. It was as if his entire body were nerve cells, all of them telling his brain about the carpet he was lying on.

He even seemed to smell things more acutely. As he struggled on the floor, he smelled a chemical odor from the carpet, as well as the acrid scent of fired ordnance. It even seemed he could smell the coppery odor of his own blood.

His hearing, too, became supersensitive. A cacophony of sound came at him.

He heard Gadgets and Julie coming from the doorway, moving forward to get a clear shot at the third man. Crazily, he wished she would stay the hell out of the firefight. He also heard a door open, down the hall, across from the terrorist with the gun. Then came the sharp, staccato blasts from the Uzis wielded by Julie and Gadgets, followed by the thud of the terrorist in the hallway staggering against the wall, then dropping to the floor.

That goddamned girl just saved my life, he thought crazily.

Another sound caught his attention.

A thump, as something hit the carpet. Even before he saw it, Lyons knew what it was.

A grenade.

He tried to roll quickly over to make certain what it was. His body refused to obey at first. Then, slowly, painfully, he managed to turn over. It was as if he were submerged in heavy oil that restricted his movements. Finally he made it, and gazed at the direction of the thump, eyes straining in the dim light.

His instincts had been right.

It was a grenade, but a flash-bang rather than a regular antipersonnel shrapnel device. The flash-bang was designed to blind and stun rather than to blow people to pieces. The idea was simple. It contained a controlled charge that released a calibrated flash of bright, white light—tens of thousands of candles, depending on the strength of the grenade—and made a simultaneous explosion.

The flash-bang contained no fragmentation or shrapnel. Its sole purpose was to immobilize, not kill.

And immobilize they would. Depending on the power and the size of the room, the effect ranged from a few seconds of blindness and ear-ringing to a near-catatonic state for several minutes, complete with ruptured eardrums and black spots in the eyes that lasted for several hours.

Lyons knew. He had used them in the past. But this was the first time he had ever been on the receiving end of one. He shouted a warning.

"Grenade!"

The sound was an unintelligible groan. His body would not, or could not, obey the message his mind demanded.

"Grenade!" he screamed again.

It was no good. He couldn't communicate with the others. When the flash-bang went off, they would be stunned into temporary paralysis, easy prey for Kadal.

The survival instinct took over.

Shot or not, if he could roll to see the grenade, he could roll away from it. Lyons summoned all his will to make the body react. Slowly—it seemed to take an eternity—he rolled back.

Turning his spine toward the grenade, Lyons covered up as best he could. He squeezed his eyes shut and pressed his face into the soft carpet. He clamped his hands over his ears, and opened his mouth to aid in equalizing the pressure on either side of his eardrums.

Get down, Julie, he thought as the grenade detonated.

The walls and floor shook with the blast. A searing ball of white light exploded into the room. Lyons was aware of the flash even through his closed eyelids, facing away from the blast, facedown in the carpet. The concussion slammed into him like a big wave.

Even as the shock washed over him, Lyons was trying again to move, to get back in the battle. He took stock of his senses.

The precautions had helped. Instead of temporarily paralyzing him, the flash had merely given a hell of a jolt to his senses. Strangely, too, he felt some of the shock from the head wound begin to fade—he could move faster than ultra slow-mo.

He looked around.

Acrid smoke drifted in layers in the dimly lit room. As he struggled to look back to where the grenade had gone off, he saw an irregular scorched patch some four feet across in the carpet. He strained to see Julie and his Able Team partners.

Nothing. Only a couple of vague shapes.

He struggled to move, to pull himself together. The body responded, but slowly. Jesus, he thought, at this rate I'll be able to crawl inside of a week.

Then he saw something else.

Movement.

Somebody was on his feet and walking around in the aftermath of the blast.

Vaguely, he made out the stocky shape in the drifting smoke.

"Pol!" he croaked. "Over here!" Again the words came out unintelligibly. At least he could make a sound, though. The figure turned toward him, gazing downward curiously.

With a jolt, Lyons realized the man wasn't Blancanales.

It was Kadal.

13

Kadal walked slowly toward Lyons.

The Ironman drove his resisting body into movement. He focused all the energies of his mind on retrieving a clip for the .45 from its pouch under his right arm. It should have been accomplished with lightning speed, but his system was still under the combined shocks of the grenade and the head wound.

Kadal raised his right arm and pointed at Lyons.

With a curious detachment, Lyons realized there was a gun in Kadal's hand. Unlike the heavy firepower that had been used so far, it was a small automatic pistol, Lyons guessed. Not much of a gun compared to the 9 mm, Lyons thought, but enough to scramble his brains.

Lyons's hand was inside his jacket, groping for a clip for the .45. But even as he tried he knew it would be too late.

The assassin raised his little pistol. A single shot rang out.

The pistol flew from Kadal's hand. He spun quickly and grabbed his arm.

A second shot split the darkness. Even though Lyons hadn't fired it, he could call it.

A miss.

The slug smacked into the wall beyond the terrorist. It shocked him into action. Without bothering to retrieve his pistol, Kadal turned and ran. He ducked down the hall and vanished into one of the rooms. Moments later, Lyons heard a door opening and wondered if it was Kadal making his escape.

The shock was wearing off. Lyons closed his fist around a clip. He slid it out of the nylon rig. Then he managed to push himself up on all fours and from there to a kneeling position. Finally, with a monumental effort, he levered himself to his feet, where he stood, bloody and swaying while the world stopped spinning.

He looked at the .45 in one hand and the clip in the other and realized that he had to load the pistol. Congratulations, Ironman, he said to himself. Good thinking.

He dumped the spent clip and inserted the fresh one, then looked around the room. Suddenly it occurred to him that the enemy was either dead or gone, and in his condition, he was in more danger from his own cocked and unlocked pistol than from anything else.

He shoved the safety back into position.

Lyons looked around for his partners. His eyes picked out two familiar human forms in the darkness. Both were on the floor, both with hands over their ears, facing away from the blast.

Most important, both were starting to move. Lyons let out a sigh of relief. Everybody was okay.

Something nudged his mind. He was forgetting something. The Ironman took a deep breath and tried to think what it might be. Then he realized there was somebody else.

"Julie!" The name burst from his lips. He realized he could talk again. "Julie! Where are you?"

Panic washed over him. He walked shakily toward the front entrance of the penthouse. Suddenly he saw her.

She lay on her side, half propped against the wall. In her right hand was a .38 Special Smith & Wesson revolver. Lyons recognized it as the standard FBI duty handgun. Her Uzi lay on the floor a few feet away.

Her eyes were shut.

"Julie!" he cried urgently as he knelt beside her.

He put his fingertips to her neck and felt. For a heart-stopping moment, there was nothing. Then he had it, and realized her heart was beating strongly. Moments later, her eyes fluttered open.

"Did I get him?" she whispered.

"Who?"

She frowned and struggled to push herself into a sitting position against the wall. "What do you mean, who? Kadal, that's who."

For the first time, Lyons added up the facts.

It had been she who had fired the shots that stopped Kadal from killing him. Gently he leaned over and took the .38 from her hand and sniffed it. Then he swung out the cylinder and confirmed the two shots fired.

"Did I get him?" she repeated.

He looked at her, feeling the moisture gather in his own eyes.

"Real close. You wounded him, and you saved my ass."

"Did he get away?"

Lyons nodded. "Don't worry, I don't think he'll get too far, especially since you shot him."

In the distance, sirens wailed above the New York predawn street noise. Lyons checked his watch. It was 3:04 A.M.

It had been 3:01 when he'd kicked the door. The whole firefight and flash-bang had consumed less than four minutes.

Six dead in four minutes of fighting.

But Kadal had escaped.

14

The President sat in the Oval Office with the Secretary of State and the Vice President. The U.S. Chief Executive scanned the dispatch on his desk. Finally he looked up and sighed.

"It doesn't look good, does it?"

"No, sir, it doesn't," replied the Secretary. He was struck by how tired the President looked. In the years they had known each other, the Secretary had come to regard the President as a man of iron constitution and even firmer will. The guy had always seemed virtually indestructible.

The events of the past two years, however, had been taking their toll.

It was no reflection on the man. Hell, the Secretary thought, a lesser man's heart would have folded from the tensions and stresses of the job. At the very least, his stomach should look like Swiss cheese.

But none of that had happened. Sure, he looked tired. But he was here, in control, calling the shots. The Secretary made a mental resolution to consider the fact the President looked tired as a sign of his strength rather than that the job was finally winning.

"Run it down for me again, if you would."

The Secretary nodded. "The Israelis, of course, are still solidly behind the Compact. Well, they're blustering about a couple of things, making some noises here and there, of course."

"Don't they always," commented the President rhetorically, more to himself than to the others.

"In any event, the commitment seems to be there on Israel's part. It's the Muslims who may be coming apart at the seams."

"How so?"

The Secretary sighed. It was the same, age-old problem. The world saw them as a homogeneous, unified group. The Muslims. In actual fact, it had become clear during the negotiations of the Tri-Lateral Compact that they were anything but that.

"Too many factions. They can't agree with one another. Then when they do agree, they don't stand by it."

"Who in particular is balking?"

The Secretary nodded. "The Shiites, of course. They're the radicals. It is my belief they are waging a systematic campaign to thwart the signing of the Tri-Lateral Compact."

"Go on."

Choosing his words carefully, the Secretary summarized it. "In terms of numbers, they're a relatively small group. But they're the militant ones. They are trying to encourage the other Muslims to pull out. And, I need not remind you, they are the ones who have commissioned the assassin, Kadal, to prevent the signing, assuming that the Shiites' other efforts at scuttling the accord fail.''

The President considered that. ''By the way, is there any progress on the progress of, uh, our people on that front?''

''No, sir. Not since the last report, which you have. They think they may have a line on where he is, but that's all.'' He sighed. ''I hope…'' He let his voice trail off.

''If anybody can do it, they can,'' said the President quietly. ''Even against a Hizbullah fanatic like Kadal.'' He paused. ''Of course, they have to find him first.''

''Yes, sir.''

Nobody spoke for several moments, while the President considered the board. Finally he spoke again.

''So what's the latest line?''

''Sir?'' The Secretary was neither a gambler nor a sports fan, and the term threw him.

''Oh. Sorry. That's bookmaker talk,'' he explained. ''I've been up to my ears in the Justice Department's reports on organized crime and gambling. After a while you start picking up the jargon. The line is the odds.'' The President allowed a wry smile. ''How many points will I have to give up to bet on the Tri-Lateral Compact going through?''

''Just an educated guess, I'd say sixty-forty.''

''Against?''

"Against. And that's assuming they can stop this Kadal business."

There was a discreet knock on the door. It announced the entry of one of the Marine adjutants attached to the White House. This meant something top priority.

"There's a call coming in on Red, sir."

"From whom?"

"Code name Stony Man, sir."

"Thank you."

The red telephone emitted a subtle chirp. The President picked it up. The others watched him closely for any sign of what was being said.

It was a brief conversation. The President listened, nodding occasionally.

"Well," he finally said, "keep at it, Hal. We're proceeding on the assumption that it's a go from this end, so I'd appreciate a report every two hours, unless something breaks one way or another before that."

He hung up the phone and turned to the others. "They had him and they lost him. They're quote hopeful unquote they will get a line on him again. They think he's wounded, at least." He turned to the Secretary. "How does that affect the line?"

The Secretary shrugged. "Oh, it doesn't, really. I can't believe he'll really go through with it. Or try to. Really, the only effect is to give a stick to the Shiites to stir the pot with, so to speak. Give a reason for doubting the Compact can work."

15

Kadal was a member of the Hizbullah. It was to them he went following his escape from the penthouse in the Towers.

His right arm throbbed. The bullet had entered on the inside of the meaty forearm, about two inches below the elbow, right where the muscle bulged outward before tapering down to the wrist. He spoke aloud as he examined the wound.

"Someday I shall find and kill that bitch."

And he was determined that when he did, it would be slowly. He would take great pleasure in it. What happened to the actress who was informing on him was nothing compared to what was going to happen to this one.

But for now, he had more immediate needs to tend to.

His contact for the Hizbullah cells in New York was Ahmed Khoury, a lawyer specializing in international law and trade.

Khoury was no less committed to the cause of the Shiites than was Kadal, and no less militant. The lawyer recognized the United States as being the best place

"Not so, John," said the President.

"What do you mean, sir?"

"They've found out that Kadal is one of them. A Shiite. Hizbullah, to be exact. This is a holy mission of revenge for him."

Now it was the Secretary's turn to look tired. "Make it seventy-thirty."

in the world to mount their campaigns and maintain their cells, because American laws were so lenient. It amused him that the Hizbullah, as sworn enemies of America, would be protected in their efforts by American laws.

The amazing thing was that usually it didn't even require corruption or coercion of the judges. With the help of defense attorneys and civil liberties unions, he was able to get cases thrown out of court by American judges using American laws.

The judges acted as if they had done something important and good, noble even, when they dismissed charges or suppressed evidence because of some meaningless point of police procedure. The American Bar Association and other lawyer's groups helped by publicly praising judges who would do this. America was truly the terrorist's haven.

Sometimes, even legal advice was free. This amused him most of all. The United States paid for its enemies to attack itself, ultimately to destroy itself.

At first he hadn't trusted those lawyers. But then he realized many of them, too, were revolutionaries, dedicated to the defense of terrorists and the destruction of the very system that created them.

America was the perfect place for his needs.

Using his considerable legal and organizational talents, combined with his zeal for Hizbullah, Ahmed Khoury had overseen the organization of a highly sophisticated and fragmented network of underground cells of followers.

They lived and trained in small squads of ten to fifteen. They were scattered throughout major cities in the U.S.; New York had the highest number. Some of them had legitimate jobs; others lived by crime. But there was one thing that bound them together—the quest for martyrdom.

To die killing the enemies of Allah.

It made no difference that in the United States they could enjoy a standard of living far better than that they had left in their native lands. Moreover, in line with revolutionaries everywhere, their cause was understood only in general terms, but without question. If it served Hizbullah, it was right, regardless of who got in the way.

No small portion of the Hizbullah power in Lebanon and elsewhere came from Ahmed Khoury's cells in New York. They raised money, purchased weapons and medical supplies and distributed propaganda. Through various political organizations, they were a not-insignificant force in manipulating the media and the legal system to retard the efforts of the CIA and the American military in combating terrorists.

They also learned to fight.

Even though many of them would never set foot in a Middle East war zone, Ahmed Khoury believed it aided morale if those in New York practiced guerrilla training, studying real tactics, using real weapons, practicing real maneuvers.

As well, it was inherent in the concept of terrorism that acts of violence could be required outside of a clearly defined fire zone at any time.

Khoury's followers of Hizbullah were trained. They learned to use M-16s and CAR-15s. They practiced with Uzis and MAC-10s and, though the live items were scarce and therefore expensive, they studied other forms of ordnance, such as LAW rockets and grenades, as well. They ran, they practiced unarmed and knife-armed combat, and tactics and concealment. And they did it because they wanted to.

Some of them enjoyed it more than others.

Those who proved themselves most suited to the methods of terrorism, and most committed to Hizbullah, might be chosen for special advanced training. The training occurred at secret camps, many of them outside the U.S., known only to Ahmed Khoury and his advisers. It was a distinction to be selected, and only a few received it.

Those who went away did not return, but went on to fight for Hizbullah in other places and ways. The rest would continue to fight and work, each in his own way, in the service of the cause.

Ahmed Khoury was a student of war, as well as of the law and the Muslim ways. He knew well that the civilian-turned-guerrilla inside the enemy lands was a force not to be ignored. The British had discovered that during the American Revolution in the years following 1776; nearly two centuries later, the U.S. had received a painful reminder in the Vietnam theater.

For Hizbullah, the struggle was eternal. It would not be over until one side or the other was eliminated.

When Kadal made contact with him, bearing the news of the American hit squad from which he had so narrowly escaped, the answer was simple.

Mobilize enough of his finest prospects to put together a retaliatory group.

Make sure they were the best.

Find the team that followed Kadal and kill them.

Then put out the word: nobody interfered with Hizbullah.

16

Just under twenty-six hours, Lyons thought as he unlocked the door to the motel room. The signing was due to take place at 10:00 A.M. the next day.

The dawn had given way to daylight. It was shortly after eight. He stepped aside to let Julie precede him, then walked in after her and locked the door.

A hasty telephone call to Brognola had set the wheels in motion to control the release of information about the incidents at Kadal's penthouse.

Lyons's hunch about Curtis had paid off, too. The big detective had been placed in charge of the case by the police commissioner himself. A preliminary statement had been released to the press, talking in suitably vague terms about a blood feud over narcotics. Lebanon, Muslims or the Tri-Lateral Compact were not mentioned anywhere. Several persons were known to have died in the predawn battle, the media reported, but further details were not known at that time.

The call to Stony Man had not been a fun one to make.

"Lyons here."

"Go ahead," directed Brognola.

"We need some juice, and we need it fast—"

"Did you get Kadal?" the Stony Man executive interrupted urgently.

"Negative. Close but not quite." Lyons's jaw jutted grimly as he conveyed the bad news.

"Is he on the streets?"

"Yes. He's probably wounded, but he's definitely ambulatory and dangerous."

Brognola accepted the news without comment. "Report," he directed calmly.

Lyons described the events that had transpired. When he had finished, Brognola moved smoothly into action.

The result was that within minutes, Curtis's men were on the scene. They processed the evidence, kept back the press and controlled the release of information.

For the time being, the killings were being attributed to an ongoing war between narcotics kingpins. Moreover, Kadal's description was being distributed under the name he had been using, Kenneth Ibrahim, as being wanted in connection with the multiple drug-related slayings at the penthouse. Any word of him would be automatically intercepted by Stony Man and the Bureau.

"We'll stand by," Lyons said as they concluded the telephone call.

"Where will you be?"

"Back at the hotel. I'm going to try to get some rest. I have a hunch he's going to surface again, but there's no use sitting around burning up nervous energy and adrenaline until he does."

"Good point. Why do you think he's going to surface?"

"Just a feeling."

"All right," said Brognola. "Go get some rest."

Inside Julie's room now, the heavy drapes kept back most of the daylight. The whisper of the air conditioner held the outside noises at bay. The atmosphere was subdued, the dimness of twilight. It seemed strangely out of kilter, because the mind and the body knew it was daytime.

The result was a strange sense of discord. Coming on the heels of little sleep, much death and a hell of a blow to the head, it gave Lyons a feeling of being displaced, a sense of being lost and lonely.

He glanced at Julie.

She was looking away from him and putting something—the key to the room, it looked like—on the low dresser. He saw her start to set it down, then stop and begin moving the other objects around—jewelry, a small notepad, some cosmetics—adjusting them, rearranging them.

He saw her profile, and saw again that she was beautiful. Then he realized that what she was doing with the stuff on the dresser was a diversion, a straw man, just something to do so she wouldn't have to look at him. He wondered if she was feeling what he was, and decided she must be.

An urgent desire for her seized him, and he turned abruptly away. He made a pretext of looking around the room, seeking a diversion himself, doing essentially the same thing she was, trying awkwardly to avoid his feelings.

For diversion, there wasn't much to work with, he realized—just your basic hotel room.

Maybe he could study the configuration of the controls on the TV, or the nonartistry of the fake, mass-produced painting on the wall, a stock autumn scene in garish oranges and browns. Absurdly an old memory struck him, a tale of a rookie agent pretending to be reading a newspaper on surveillance in a train station, a paper he had grabbed off the bench next to him. But the paper had been printed in Hebrew, and it didn't have any pictures, and the young secret squirrel hadn't known he was holding it upside down.

Then Lyons remembered his pleasant speculation on the matter of what Julie might have been wearing as she slept. Always the trained observer, Lyons thought ruefully as he caught himself scanning the room for a nightgown.

I feel like a goddamned Peeping Tom, he thought. Still, it gave him something to do rather than feel the emotions within him.

For about two seconds, anyway.

He was gratified that he didn't see anything that looked like sleepwear. The speculation became more pleasant and more immediate, and then suddenly it was wholly inadequate to divert him from the needs he felt.

"What's the matter?" She spoke without turning away from the dresser.

He gave a start. "What do you mean?"

"What are you thinking about? Is something wrong?"

"No. Why?"

She turned to look at him, her eyes wide and dark, her face clouded with emotion. "Oh, I don't know. You just had kind of a funny look on your face. That's all."

"Yeah." His voice was hoarse and low. It was all he could think of to say. "Funny."

Julie took two steps and stood before him. She started to reach up, hesitated, then touched the corners of his eyes with her hand, first one side, then the other.

"Tired eyes," she said softly as she traced the creases.

"Yeah. Tired."

Desire suddenly became need. It was almost tangible in its immediacy, irresistible.

He was bone tired. His head had two stitches on top of a hell of a bruise. It made a burning on top of an ache, but he had refused any painkillers on the theory that if they got another line on Kadal, he would need to be fully alert.

In the preceding hours, he had killed and nearly been killed. Somewhere out there the world's most formidable assassin was on the loose, wounded, preparing to kill again.

God, how he wanted her.

Abstractedly, knowing he was stalling, Lyons wondered if he wanted her for herself, or for some other reason—what she symbolized.

Or did it matter? He longed for life, for the ability to *feel*, to give and receive something besides death. And the battles they had just been through and that he knew were coming. What did that have to do with his feelings? Could it be that some atavistic mechanism within them, some primitive program for survival, increased their desire when faced with death?

He felt a sudden shame, almost a guilt. If that theory was true, he wondered if he would be using her, committing a taking without a giving.

He was stalling, and they both knew it. Her eyes were serious, dark and deep, smoky windows of emotion so exquisite that his breath caught in his chest. Then at last he allowed himself to see his own desire mirrored in her eyes.

Awkwardly he reached for her.

She went to him eagerly and pressed herself against him, putting her arms around his neck, clinging to him. It seemed as if she was somehow gripping him everywhere they touched, as though even the surfaces of her arms and thighs and body could clutch him and hold him. They kissed deeply, compulsively, tasting

Meet America's most potent human weapons

Mack Bolan and his courageous combat squads—*Able Team & Phoenix Force*—along with *SOBs* and *Vietnam: Ground Zero* unleash the best sharpshooting firepower ever published. Join them as they blast their way through page after page of raw action toward a fiery climax of rage and retribution.

each other's warmth. Then she slid her lips to his ear, whispering and sighing words of love.

He buried his face in her hair and inhaled the scents that mingled there, sweet and warm and alive. Her fingers gripped the back of his neck and the thick muscles of his trapezius, squeezing, kneading, pinching. Her breath seared his face, his neck and his ear with a long, shuddering gasp.

His hands moved from her shoulders down her back to her sides. He stroked her, squeezed her, dragging his fingernails along her body beneath the light shirt. His fingertips found the side of her breast, and he scratched lightly, first over her bra, then tracing her skin along its borders. Then clumsily he was fumbling with the buttons of her blouse, parting it, sliding the roughness of his hands along the satin surfaces of her flesh.

A moan escaped her, and she fastened her mouth to his neck with an urgent suction.

Her nipples were erect and tight under the brassiere. Then she helped him open it, and with a gesture of exquisite femininity, moved her shoulders forward to free her breasts from the fabric cups. He moved his thumbs across puckered flesh, feeling her heat, gently lifting the weight of her breasts, then bending forward and sliding his lips down her neck, down the smooth flesh until they fastened onto a nipple.

He felt her hands down his sides, then across the ridges of his stomach to rub him through the heavy fabric of his pants. Then her fingers stormed his belt and the buttons below it. Moments later, their clothes were in a tangled pile on the floor, and she sank back on the bed, reaching for him, pulling him to her in the artificial twilight.

Her skin burned him, inflamed him, and he lowered himself over her. She made a sound that was half sigh, half whimper. He supported his weight on his hands and knees and lightly stroked her body with his own, grazing his chest against hers, brushing her face with his nose and lips. Then she gripped him and opened herself to him, guiding him slowly, gently inside her, a wonderful silky joining of their bodies.

And more. They moved together, at first slowly and languidly, then with increasing tempo as together they built and held and finally peaked in a shuddering celebration of human emotion.

A long time later, as they lay still joined, she stirred in his arms. Their eyes met and held on to each other. Finally she let out a long sigh and spoke a single word of contentment.

"Golly."

He smiled. "Yeah."

"That was nice."

"Yeah." He spoke in a low, satisfied sigh.

"Is that all you can say?" she teased.

"Yeah."

She smiled and kissed him. A few moments later, she spoke up again.

"Carl?"

"Yeah?"

"What'll we tell the others we did?"

He thought about it. "Don't tell them anything."

She nodded, then laughed. "No. I'll tell them I rested."

"Rested?"

"Yeah. Rested. That's what we did."

He looked at her and grinned. "I like your way of resting, lady."

"Me, too."

"I think we should try to get a lot of rest, you know?"

She smiled. "I agree. Starting now."

"Starting now," he said nodding and moving his lips onto hers.

At that moment, the telephone shrilled on the nightstand. Before he even answered it, Lyons knew what it would be about.

Kadal.

They had found him.

The dream was about to be confronted. The hand was going to be played out. The last card would be turned up.

Six ways to lose. Six ways to die.

But a lot of ways to live, to win, also. And one thing was sure. He might lose, but he would never be beaten.

Besides, Lyons thought, I've been "resting." You guys don't have a chance now.

He reached for the telephone. "Lyons here." He listened, then his gaze met Julie's. He saw the question in her eyes and nodded.

Wordlessly she pushed up to a sitting position, then turned away from him to sit on the edge of the bed and reach for her clothes, which lay in a heap on the floor. Something about the way she had turned as she sat up—maybe it was slightly hurried—had a curiously touching modesty to it, especially considering the intimacies of the preceding two hours.

Part of his mind listened to the official voice on the telephone. Another part wondered if he loved her.

He nodded into the phone. "Roger. We're en route."

He hung up and got out of bed. During the entire conversation on the telephone, he'd spoken only six words. He added five more.

"Time to go to work."

17

On the streets they called it "the ruins."

Occupying a mile or so of warehouses and docks in the worst part of the waterfront, the ruins had the look of an apocalyptic war zone. Bigger ships and newer docks had taken the major trade away from the ruins, and the property was not worth taking over for anything else.

It lay largely abandoned now, except for rats, wild dogs and a handful of society's castoffs to whom the area appealed as a place to live. Occasionally a warehouse was in use by some industrial company or another, usually for storage of unused equipment, but that was the exception rather than the rule.

Even the cops stayed out of the area. No one, it seemed, cared what happened down there.

Lyons guided the van along a path that took them generally in a southeasterly direction. Toward the ruins.

"So how'd they get onto him, anyway?" inquired Gadgets.

He and Blancanales had returned to Kadal's penthouse after taking Lyons to the hospital and then dropping him and Julie back at the hotel.

They had wanted to be on hand in case any lead to Kadal's whereabouts cropped up among the contents of the penthouse. Accordingly, together with a member of the FBI's Middle East Terrorist Unit, they stood by while Curtis's detectives processed the scene. They were still there when the call had come through that Kadal had been sighted at the ruins.

If either Gadgets or Blancanales guessed how Lyons and Julie had spent the morning, neither ventured to comment on it. The closest thing to it was a casual question by the Politician as they met up.

"So what'd you do back at the motel?"

There had been no hint of needling, no knowing wink or leer.

Lyons shrugged. "Nothing much. Just kicked back, mainly."

Julie nodded. "Rested," she added.

Lyons suppressed a smile at her use of the term.

"You feel okay?" Blancanales directed tne question at Lyons.

"Yeah."

Now, in response to Gadgets's question about how the trail had been picked up, Lyons relayed what he had been told in the call from Brognola.

"It's the goddamnedest thing," he began.

"So tell us."

"Remember what we learned at the briefing at Stony Man, about how the squad Julie was assigned to had him under surveillance?"

Blancanales nodded. "Sure. They had an informant into him."

"Right. And remember what Kadal did to her. Found her out and delivered her head in a box. Two boxes, actually. One the taxidermy'ed version, the other containing the leftovers."

"Yeah. We remember. What's that have to do with this?"

"Seems there was another guy on the squad. A CIA man named Harper. He had been opposed to the mission, apparently. He wanted to pull out the informant and nuke Kadal then and there."

"At least somebody in that operation had some sense," muttered Blancanales, forgetting that Julie had been in on it, too. Then he remembered, and added hastily, "In addition to present company, of course."

She smiled but said nothing, recalling her own disagreements with Harper on the subject of assassination as a tool of international diplomacy. *Albeit a defensive one, in our case,* she told herself. Then honesty got the best of her, and she spoke up.

"Actually, I rather liked Harper. He had a lot more experience than any of the rest of us, and as it turned out, he was right."

"It happens," responded the Politician.

The young FBI agent shook her head. "I have to admit that I was one of the ones who disagreed with him at the time. We were wrong. What can I say?"

"No need to say anything," Lyons responded equably. "We're here, and that's that. The rest is history."

"True enough," agreed Blancanales.

"At any rate," Lyons continued, "it seems that after Source One arrived in two pieces, Harper went off the deep end."

"What happened?"

"He wigged out. Dropped out of sight. And now we learn that he had gone off on his own unofficial search and destroy of Kadal, by himself."

"And?" prompted Julie this time. This was the first she had heard of the details.

"You can't fault his approach. He somehow tumbled to the fact that you were hooked up with us—" Lyons gestured at Julie as he spoke "—and so he began following us."

Julie looked puzzled. "Why? Did he think we'd lead him to Kadal?"

"That's my guess. Then when we lost Kadal at the Towers, Harper was hovering in the background. He saw Kadal come out, and we didn't, so he tailed him to this hellhole called the ruins and put in a call that he knew would get to us."

They thought that over. After a moment, Blancanales spoke.

"What's he going to do now? Try to throw in with us?"

Lyons shook his head. "In theory, no. The word is he's going to pull out and let us have him."

"Doesn't sound very plausible for a guy who's wigged," observed Gadgets.

"No, it doesn't, does it."

BY THREE O'CLOCK, they arrived at the ruins.

A paved access road was generally regarded as the unofficial boundary of the area. For the most part it ran parallel to the shoreline, about three-quarters of a mile back from it.

Between the road and the harbor lay the wasteland that held their quarry.

Along the access road squatted warehouse after warehouse. All of them were empty. Some of them were gutted, and a couple had been demolished to piles of rubble and half-standing walls. Dirty brown brick and gray cement, they sat in abject desolation beneath the dull gray sky.

Beyond the warehouses lay a handful of smaller buildings and countless hulks of abandoned machinery and junked cars. In some cases, the pieces of equipment and the piles of cars reached twenty feet high. It made a patchy metallic jungle that stretched southeast almost to the docks.

In the middle of it was a black pool maybe fifty feet across, ringed by a tattered chain-link fence. Oil or industrial waste of some sort, it looked like.

Lyons brought the van to a stop just as the area came into sight. He pulled off the access road, and they surveyed the lonely tableau.

"Jesus," whispered Gadgets reverently, "it looks like World War III has come and gone. After the Apocalypse."

"Goddamned godforsaken place," muttered Lyons in agreement.

The Ironman remembered visiting some uninhabited places in South America, and thinking that it had to be the loneliest place in the world. Somehow, though, this looked even worse. Perhaps it was because here the ruined and empty buildings served as a reminder that man had once been here, but had abandoned it. It heightened rather than reduced the emptiness.

There is nothing here for you, the area seemed to say. Nothing but decline and death and decay. Man is gone. All that remains is the ruins.

And Death.

Lyons's eyes narrowed. He had an appointment to keep, a hand of blackjack to play out. The desolation was making his stomach crawl as it was. When he got those feelings, which was rare, though not as rare as it used to be, he had a simple solution.

Attack.

Swing into action. Get the show on the road. Or else pack up your tent and go home. But for Pete's sake, do something—don't just sit there and finger your psyche.

Do it scared if you have to, but nut up and goddamn do it.

"We've got a fight to fight," he said. "Let's get on with it."

"Sure, Ironman," said Gadgets easily. "Whenever you're ready."

"I'm ready now."

"Then let's do it."

Blancanales interjected a tactical question. "Just where in this shit hole is he supposed to be? If we don't have some idea, maybe we ought to call in some support."

Lyons shook his head. "No time. Besides, according to Harper, he's in one of the warehouses just north of the biggest one."

"What's he doing here, anyway?"

"Harper thinks it's, quote, where these Hizbullah scumbags hang out, unquote. He says they have a kind of training or headquarters here for some of their cells in New York. He thinks Kadal is hooking up with reinforcements."

"Great." Gadgets wrenched the handle to the sliding door on the side of the van and slid it open.

Once again the weaponry started with pistols, the Kissinger-approved .45s. This time, though, the main weaponry went beyond the Uzi auto-pistols.

Gadgets handed each of the men an M-16 assault rifle. He held one up to Julie, his eyes questioning. She hesitated a moment, then accepted it. Lyons watched as she checked the selector switch, found it on full-auto and pushed it to semi.

Smart lady, he thought. She's handled one before, and knows it's tough to control on auto-burn. Still, even on semi-auto, she's got a lot more firepower than with the Uzi.

Especially for this shit, he thought, looking at the ruins.

Gadgets also passed light packs to Blancanales and Lyons. Extra clips, grenades—both fragmentation and flash-bang—and hand-held radios were inside the packs.

The preparations were made in silence. Finally Blancanales spoke again.

"How do you want to make the approach?"

Lyons surveyed the layout. "I think we can drive to the closest warehouse," he said, pointing. "From there, it's on foot."

"Roger."

"Any questions?" Lyons looked at the small group.

There weren't any.

The Ironman glanced at Julie. Her face was tight and a little pale. He started to give her another chance to hold back, then checked himself.

He knew what the response would be: I can handle it.

She probably could, at that.

"All right," he said aloud, "let's get to it."

18

Lyons coasted the van to a stop near the loading dock of the first warehouse.

The building was forty feet tall. Dirty, crumbling cement covered the exterior of the first story, and at this stage of its existence, even the old graffiti was barely visible. A ramp of broken pavement led to the loading dock where Lyons had parked. Elsewhere, the dirt adjacent to the warehouse was so soaked with years of oil that it was stained a permanent petroleum brown.

As he put the van into Park, Lyons saw something glint in the hazy afternoon light. The glint came from beyond the warehouse.

Nothing, but nothing, was shiny in this godforsaken place, Lyons thought. This could only mean trouble.

"Out and down!" he yelled, bailing out of the van. The others followed and, weapons in hand, jogged to the wall of the warehouse.

An instant later the van exploded into an orange oily ball of flame.

"Take cover!" Lyons shouted. Ahead of him, before the gaping openings used for loading and unloading equipment, was a standard-size door.

He sprinted for it.

He grabbed the knob and twisted. Surprisingly the door was locked. For an instant he considered dashing ahead for one of the bigger openings. Instinct, however, told him not to. Over the years those instincts had generally been right, and he paid attention to this one.

The Ironman threw a shoulder against the door. It yielded, and he tumbled inside, Blancanales and Julie at his heels. Gadgets was nowhere to be seen.

A pang of fear struck him. Had something happened to their third man?

He didn't have time to worry. A swarthy figure loomed, raising an Uzi-type assault rifle.

"Look out!" yelled Blancanales.

The warning was unnecessary.

Lyons clamped the M-16 against his hip and unleashed a burst.

At the fifteen-odd feet that separated Lyons from his target, the .223 projectiles would be moving at some three thousand feet per second. The impact swatted the man away like a fly, hurling him backward. He hit the dirty cement and rolled twice, leaving bright red streaks on the floor.

Lyons took stock of their location. They were in an anteroom of sorts, probably an office or receiving area back when the warehouse had been in use. It was small compared to the rest of the warehouse; Lyons estimated it at maybe twenty by thirty. Beyond the dead man double doors led into the warehouse itself.

Again, his instinct told him to move.

Lyons obeyed and dashed ahead for the doors.

As he neared the doors, he could see the massive iron frame of a giant piece of equipment, a metal press of some sort, he guessed. It squatted on the pavement, ponderous and solid, some fifteen feet inside, beyond the doors. The main cavern of the gutted building opened off to the left, making the piece of equipment perfect cover.

The Ironman didn't hesitate. He sprinted through the doorway. Two strides inside he launched himself forward in a long, flat dive.

The dive saved the Ironman's life. His reckless charge probably saved all their lives.

In his peripheral vision as he dived, Lyons got a glimpse of what awaited them if they had dashed ahead into the bigger opening. At least fifteen men with automatic weapons were positioned behind covering piles of rubble. Their backs were to him. Their attention was focused on the large opening of the warehouse, the one Lyons and the others would have gone through had he not heeded his gut feelings.

It would have been a shooting gallery, with Able Team as targets.

The ambushers were starting to turn now. There had been a moment's inaction, Lyons knew, when his gunfire took them by surprise as he shot the man in the office.

One of the closer soldiers rolled to one side and fired off a burst as Lyons dived forward. The 9 mm slugs cut the air above where the Ironman had been a moment before.

When you're hot, you're hot, thought Lyons exultantly.

He bounded to his feet and snared a fragmentation grenade from the pouch at his waist. In less than a second he'd lobbed it over the machine.

The arc and the timing were perfect. The cement floor of the warehouse shook as the blast reverberated in the cavernous structure. A hail of shrapnel peppered the men scrambling to change their positions to meet the threat behind them.

Before the shock waves had time to diminish, Lyons stepped out from the cover of the huge press, M-16 clamped against his hip.

It was auto-burn all the way.

A savage yell tore from his throat. It rose above the hammering of the M-16 as he swung the weapon from side to side, his feet planted, knees slightly bent, twisting his body at the waist.

A commando not twenty feet away was trying to scramble to his feet. He was in a crouch when Lyons fired. Three thousand f.p.s. and twelve hundred foot-pounds of energy slammed into his head, which disintegrated like an overripe melon.

The man next to him was ready to fire. Two rounds hit him in the midsection, and he folded over.

Lyons swung the stream of death like a firehose, washing out the enemy in a fast swipe. Suddenly there was a clank, and the M-16 locked open, magazine empty.

Still the deadly hammering continued. Still the Shiite terrorists bucked in the hail of fire.

Pol! he thought excitedly.

The former Green Beret was standing in the doorway to the room they had come into, working his own M-16 with the same skill Lyons had shown.

The Ironman grabbed for the empty magazine and twisted it free. The weapon radiated heat from the sustained fire. Lyons tossed the empty mag and rammed in a fresh one, slamming it home with the heel of his hand and simultaneously releasing the slide. It shut with a hard, metallic clank, and he was back in business.

There was nobody to do business with. Or to.

He stood, M-16 ready, alert for any new threat, or anyone playing possum.

None showed.

Here and there one of the terrorists, wounded but not dead, moved. But it was the stirring of grievously injured men, not the sudden motion of an attack.

"Pol!"

"*Sí, amigo!*"

"Cover me!"

"You got it!"

Lyons stepped warily forward to the rubble that the ambushers had used as cover. Slowly he moved down the line, examining the dead, searching for any living.

He stopped and looked closely at one, a stocky man in his twenties. The man was still alive.

Lyons lowered the muzzle of the M-16 to the guy's head. When the Ironman realized the guy wouldn't last another few minutes, he moved on to the next one.

In spite of the slight ringing in their ears from the firefight, Lyons's senses felt supertuned, hypersensitive from the combat. As a result, he was able to hear the feminine gasp from near where Pol stood.

It amused him in a way that was not condescending. Julie had a hell of a lot of potential, and she had saved his ass back at the penthouse. But she was still green in the killing business, still an accomplished amateur.

Suddenly a bloody form surged up not three feet from him. The Uzi in the commando's hands swung toward the Ironman.

The terrorist was too close to Lyons for Blancanales to shoot.

Lyons reacted instantly, swinging the barrel of the M-16 and knocking the weapon from the commando's hands. The impact staggered the terrorist, who took two shaky steps and fell to the cement floor on all fours.

Lyons swung his gun down, ready to put one into the man's head. Then, with a jolt, he realized the man was a woman.

Warily he squatted, carefully checking for other weapons or a grenade. Seeing neither, he put his hand under the woman's chin and lifted her face to him.

It was a dark, pretty face under the blood and the pain.

"Kadal," said Lyons. "Where is he?"

The woman was silent.

"Where is he?" Lyons repeated, louder this time.

Her eyes blazed hatred. "You will die!" she spat. "All of you. Kadal and the others will kill you like dogs!"

Lyons reached down and gripped the terrorist's jaw between his thumb and forefinger. He clamped his hand down in a steely grip and half-lifted her face up to his.

"Listen," he grated between clenched teeth. "You can have it hard, or you can have it easy. You're dead meat either way."

Between his grip the girl snarled her reply. "Fuck you, pig."

"Pol!" Lyons shouted over his shoulder.

"Yo."

"Why don't you take a stroll? Maybe go try to hook up with Gadgets." Even as he spoke, Lyons saw their third man approaching from the rear of the cavernous warehouse. Relieved, he amended the suggestion. "Just walk around for a while."

"Got it."

Blancanales took Julie's arm and guided her out through the small office. They walked past the smoking remains of the van and stood looking northwest at the New York skyline.

"What's he going to do?" The voice beside him was small, almost forlorn.

The Politician didn't respond.

"Is he going to torture her?"

Blancanales gazed at the dirty gray skyline and weighed her question. Finally he looked at her beautiful, troubled face for a long moment, then looked away again.

A strange silence surrounded them, an eerie absence of the small background noises so ordinary that the ear normally ignores them. Far away, behind them, came the low hoot of a ship. The weak sun filtered through the gray clouds. The smell of old oil hung in the air.

When Blancanales finally spoke, his voice was soft. "You love him, don't you?"

It was her turn for silence. "I don't know," she said at last.

"I do. It shows."

She sighed. "Yes. I guess I do."

"Then you don't need to know what you asked."

"I think I do."

But Blancanales shook his head again. He looked at her, his lined face gentle. "He will do what he has to do. If it's right, he'll do it, no matter how hard it is on him. He's that way."

"Nothing makes *that* right." Her voice was despairing rather than angry. "Nothing."

"If you were being held captive, and that girl knew where, you might feel differently," observed the Politician gently.

She thought that over. "I wonder if he would do it in that case."

Blancanales nodded. "He would." There was not a trace of doubt in his voice.

"How do you know?"

"He is one of my three best friends on this earth. I know him. I know he would. Because he loves you."

Julie turned away and stood, arms across her chest, hugging herself, tears burning in her eyes.

Alone in the ruins.

19

Lyons stood up from the dead Hizbullah fighter, the woman. He looked around and saw only Gadgets. His Able Team partner was standing about twenty feet away, leaning against the massive metal monster behind which Lyons had first sought cover. Schwarz watched without comment as Lyons wiped his hands on his pant legs.

The Ironman raised an inquiring eyebrow. Gadgets knew what he was asking.

"Outside," he said simply.

Lyons nodded and walked through the yawning entrance of the abandoned structure. Blancanales and Julie were standing near the smoldering van.

He noticed that Julie had her back to them. Her arms were clutched across her chest, hugging herself, her back rounded. Gadgets stood next to her, a few feet away, looking at the ground.

The Ironman pushed the turmoil of emotions from his mind. They had work to do, a man to meet, a hand to play out. Time enough for the personal touch later, providing he remained alive. And if he didn't, it wouldn't matter.

"According to the woman, there's a tunnel at the back of the warehouse," Lyons announced, striding over to them.

"Where does it go?" inquired Blancanales.

"They've got some underground setup down there. She wasn't clear on the details."

"Is Kadal here?"

"Yes. At least he was, unless he got away."

Blancanales shrugged. "You call it, amigo."

Lyons jerked his head toward the rear of the warehouse. "Let's go." He turned to Julie, who hadn't looked at him the entire time. "Julie?" he said gently, oblivious of the others.

"Yes." She still averted her gaze.

"You okay?"

She nodded.

"You in?"

She hesitated, then lifted her head and looked at him. "I'm in," she said flatly. "Let's go."

Lyons examined her features for any clue of what she was thinking, or any sign of...affection. There was none of either. Well, that should tell him something.

"All right," he said, his voice all business. "Let's go."

It's a hell of a note, he thought angrily, to be going into battle with your mind filled with all this emotional crap. Whoever it was that said they're all 98.6 inside had the right idea.

He knew it was a lie even as he thought it.

They found the entrance to the tunnel in the dirty basement of the warehouse. It was a hole that went straight into the earth behind the basement wall. The three men had flashlights from their packs; only Lyons switched his on.

The tunnel went straight ahead for the first five yards or so. Then it made what was nearly a right angle, and sloped sharply, nearly vertically downward. Lyons estimated the slope at sixty or seventy degrees.

There was no ladder. A heavy woven nylon rope and a length of red three-quarter-inch nylon webbing were secured to a heavy bolt that jutted up from the rock floor just before the shaft started downward. The two lines disappeared into the darkness of the shaft.

Both looked new.

Blancanales tested them. "Solid," he observed.

Gadgets looked at Lyons. "Well?"

"I say yes," said the Ironman.

Nobody disagreed. Twelve minutes later they were all down at the bottom of the vertical shaft.

Darkness surrounded them. The angle of the shaft blocked any light that filtered from the basement, which was precious little anyway. The dark brown of creosoted timbers seemed to absorb the light, so any reflection was minimal or nonexistent. If one were standing at the bottom looking up, all that was visible even with the flashlight off was a faint, diffused glow.

The place felt like an unused tomb in the dead of night.

"Dios!" muttered Blancanales as the darkness closed in about them. The heavy subterranean silence bounced his hoarse voice back in what seemed a hostile echo.

"Amen!" Julie whispered. Even Lyons was affected by the gloom of the place.

The bottom of the initial shaft, where they now stood, opened to a cavern the size of a long living room. At the far end, the cavern narrowed to a horizontal shaft or tunnel that disappeared into the darkness.

Heavy timbers shored the walls and ceiling at the far end, just before the room narrowed to the tunnel. Some were massive and old, their surfaces rough and splintery. These were reinforced and cross braced with newer timbers, sturdy and by comparison smooth. Here and there, the bracing was done by steel beams.

Gadgets gestured at the cross bracing with his flashlight. "It looks like there may have been another shaft, or a hole of some kind from the surface. It may have been an entrance, and caved in."

"What do you think it was used for?" Julie inquired in a hushed whisper.

"The tunnel?"

She nodded.

Lyons shrugged. "Who knows? I can't imagine why they needed tunnels connecting warehouses. But, hell, this whole area could be filled with shafts, for all we know."

From where they stood, the shaft was nearly horizontal, with only a slight downward slope. Here, the tunnel looked well shored, with new wood braces interspersed with an occasional steel one. The floor was free of debris, and showed signs of recent foot traffic.

"What do you suppose this is?" whispered Julie. "It's obviously not abandoned like the rest of the stuff above, the ruins."

Lyons nodded. "If I had to guess, I would say this is used in some way by the Hizbullah, or one of the local cells."

"What for?"

"Storage, probably. Munitions. Supplies. Your general terrorist larder."

"Well," she observed, "it's an ideal place for it, buried in the middle of the city practically."

They moved on down the shaft. After a few moments, Gadgets spoke up. "I wonder what would happen down here if somebody starts shooting."

"Don't," replied Lyons.

"Don't shoot?"

"No. Don't wonder. If we have to shoot it out, we'll shoot. If it caves in, it caves in."

Blancanales grinned in the darkness. They were in the battle mode again—no more doubts, just "nut up" and go for it—win, lose or draw. "Life's a bitch," he said jauntily.

"And then you die," shot back Lyons as he turned and swung off down the tunnel.

In most places, the tunnel was easily high enough for a person to stand upright. With Lyons in the lead, followed by Gadgets and Julie, Blancanales bringing up the rear, they set off at a brisk patrolling pace.

"Hold it!" Lyons commanded suddenly.

"What is it?" inquired Blancanales from the rear.

"I think we're getting close."

"How so?"

Lyons shook his head. "I don't know exactly. Maybe I heard something, or maybe it's just a hunch."

Gadgets nodded. "I was thinking the same thing," he said.

"What we need," the Ironman said pensively, "is a ruse. Something to draw them out. Draw their fire." He was tempted to wisecrack about sending Julie, as the rookie, down the tunnel, but figured this wasn't the time or place for it. Besides, it might sound sexist.

Then an idea hit him. "Stand by," he said softly. "Stay put, but be ready for anything."

He moved noisily ahead, striding down the tunnel. The others heard the clink of his weaponry, the nylon rustle of clothing and gear and heavy footsteps. Then his voice bounced off the walls in a heavy, loud whisper.

"All right, guys. Let's get this over with. Move out."

More heavy footfalls and the sound of a dislodged rock reached them. Then his flashlight came on some forty feet ahead of them—they could see the backlight as he shined it up ahead at a curve in the tunnel.

He moved it from side to side and up and down as he marched in place, simulating what somebody down the shaft would see if he were walking toward them. From behind him, his partners could see a bend in the tunnel some fifteen or twenty feet ahead of Lyons.

"Hold it!" Lyons commanded again, in the same stage whisper.

He doused the light. At the same time, a rock tumbled noisily along the path of the tunnel, ahead and around the bend, thrown by the Ironman.

Lyons turned and sprinted back up the tunnel toward his partners.

The response was instantaneous.

A vivid flame roiled out at them from around the bend. It was accompanied by the heavy petrochemical stench of a flame thrower.

Bright orange lit up the curve in the tunnel. The fireball bounced off the wall and surged up the shaft. Even at their distance, they felt the searing heat blast the exposed skin of their hands and faces.

"Back!" shouted Lyons over the roar of the flame thrower. He wrenched the .45 from his shoulder holster and fired five times in the direction of the flames. Lead spattered against stone. Ricochets sang off into the darkness.

A single sharp cry of pain followed. It was followed immediately by a fusillade of shots from around the bend up ahead. The Able members looked at one another.

The terrorists were firing automatic weapons, heedless of the danger of a cave-in.

The shots blended together. They made a single thunderous roll that reverberated off the tunnel walls. Hot lead fragments and chips of rock peppered the confined space.

Far in the distance, behind them, came a low, indistinct rumble. The rock beneath their feet gave an almost imperceptible movement.

"Cave-in!" This came from Gadgets. "Holy shit, Ironman..."

He didn't have a chance to finish. Another ball of flame roared up the tunnel at them. No sooner had it subsided than a fire team of four terrorists burst around the bend, automatic weapons poised and ready.

Able Team raised their weapons.

Two choices.

Shoot now and run the risk of a cave-in. Or try to beat a retreat and die like dogs, shot by the maniacs ahead who either didn't know or didn't care if the place fell in.

The response was instantaneous. And unanimous.

Lyons and Blancanales, in front, opened fire the instant the terrorists did. The thunder of gunfire echoed and reechoed up and down the tunnel. It seemed to take a long time to die out.

Finally it did.

The four terrorists lay dead or dying on the floor of the tunnel, their bodies sprawled on the hard rock floor.

Lyons touched the outside of his Kevlar vest where he had taken two slugs below the rib cage on the right side. There was no penetration, he could tell, thanks to the body armor. He did have a hell of a bruise, though.

"Everybody okay?" he inquired of the others. "Report."

He turned around as he spoke. Even as he turned, he knew everybody wasn't okay.

Julie was down.

She half sat, half lay against the side of the tunnel. The left side of her body armor was drenched in blood that seemed to be coming from the area of her armpit.

"Julie!"

He cried out the name, fighting a panic that was completely irrational—and, he knew, unforgivable in a professional soldier—as he knelt quickly by her. The one Achilles' heel of body armor was the side area, particularly the armpit, if the vest was too big.

Velcro crackled as he eased the straps away to inspect the damage.

It looked bad.

It might be, and it might not be, of course. It all depended where the bullets went after they entered the body.

He found the entrance wound, a neat, round hole in the satiny flesh that only hours before he had caressed with his lips. It was a few inches below her armpit and toward the back. In the light of his flash, it made a small, dark spot on the white skin.

Suddenly the ground shook again. This time it was less violent, but it lasted longer. When the movement stopped, the sound of rock falling reached them. It came from behind, along the path they had just traveled.

"Pol! Gadgets! Go check out the tunnel! See if we can get out!"

The two men sprinted back up the shaft. Lyons turned his attention to the still form on the ground.

"Julie!" he said urgently.

There was no response. Her face was pale and pinched, small and vulnerable. Lyons mentally cursed himself for allowing her to accompany the group to that subterranean hell.

"Julie! Can you hear me?"

Her eyes fluttered open and met his. Her tongue moved across her lips, moistening them. Then with a faint smile, she whispered, "Speak up, Carl. I can't hear you."

Relief flooded over him. "Can you walk?"

"I can run if I have to."

"How does it feel?"

Again, she forced a smile. "My nerves are shot."

"Come on," said Lyons abruptly, "stand up." He picked her easily up and set her on her feet.

At that moment, the ground shook again. Julie staggered and nearly fell. A heavy rumbling echoed down the tunnel, followed by the unmistakable sound of a rockslide.

Lyons snatched Julie into his arms and sprinted back up the tunnel in the direction Blancanales and Gadgets had gone.

Thirty feet ahead of him, the roof of the tunnel collapsed in a thunderous roar of falling rock, sealing off the passageway with a ton of granite.

20

The noise from the cave-in died away gradually.

His chin tucked by his right shoulder, the knit shirt pulled over his nose to act as a crude filter, Lyons shone his flashlight up the tunnel.

The dust eddied and swirled in the bright beam. Through it, a wall of broken rock and boulders rose before them.

Solid. Impenetrable.

Lyons stared at it, his mind unwilling to accept the message his eyes were sending. Beside him, Julie coughed and choked on the dust. Then he heard her breath catch as she saw their fate.

"Oh, my God," she said.

"No shit."

He walked forward to the pile of rubble and examined it. He stood there for several long seconds. Then Julie's voice came to him.

"Solid?"

"Solid." As he spoke, Lyons wondered if Gadgets and Blancanales had made it.

There were three possibilities, as he saw it. One, they could be buried in the very pile he was looking at, entombed forever only a few feet from where he now stood. Or they could be beyond it, trapped by yet another cave-in still farther ahead, doomed to die like rats in a rock-walled cell. Or maybe they had made it out.

He might never know.

"Well, hell," he said, trying to sound more fatalistic than he felt.

"Now what?"

He thought for a moment. Then it struck him. "Look at it this way. Either we'll get out some other way..."

"Or?"

"Or we won." He turned to face her, shining the light against the wall so the indirect light reflected onto them.

He saw her frown in the semidarkness. "How do you figure that?"

"Presumably this tunnel leads somewhere, or Kadal wouldn't have come down here in the first place."

"Unless it was another ambush," she pointed out.

"Okay, there's that. But that isn't too likely. I'll bet—"

"Or unless there was another cave-in in that direction, as well," she interjected.

Lyons gave an exasperated huff. "Julie," he said, his voice half sharp, half sarcastic, "sweetheart. Baby. Listen to me. What I'm trying to say is this. If there's no way out—for whatever reason—then Kadal can't get out, either. Any more than we can." He paused.

She didn't respond.

"And if he can't get out, he can't kill a bunch of people at the signing of the Tri-Lateral Compact. That means we win. We accomplished the mission."

"Great."

His face creased in a smile, and he reached out and touched her cheek with the back of his index finger. "Don't snivel. Nobody said it would be easy." He spoke gently, using the tone of his voice along with the smile to soften the impact of his words.

She returned the smile. "Life's a bitch...."

"Right. And then you die. But there's another possibility, too. Could be there's still a way out. And if there is, our mission isn't over yet. We've still got to catch up to Kadal, but at least it means we get out."

Julie thought that over. "So if he's got a way out, so do we, but we still have to find him and kill him." She said the words without a second's hesitation. "And if there isn't, we've won, in a sense."

"Right on."

"Yeah."

"So what's the plan?"

Lyons pointed back down the tunnel. "I vote we go that way. If you can walk, that is."

"You're on. And I can walk. For now, anyway."

They retraced their steps back down the shaft. They passed the spot where Julie had been hit. Up ahead was the place where Lyons had made his ruse; beyond that were the dead from Kadal's fire team.

They moved forward.

A long groan that sounded as if it came from the depths of hell rent the tomblike silence. It started as a low moan, then rose in an acceleration of suffering, only to fall off into silence. It was a young, clear voice—under other circumstances, and in another key, it could have been a musical voice. As it was, it sounded like a tortured demon.

It came from the bodies ahead of them.

Lyons extinguished the light and flattened them quickly, instinctively, against the wall.

And listened.

Had Kadal abandoned his wounded? Or was it a trap?

The groan rose and fell again. It raised the hair on their necks and left a queasy tingle in the pits of their stomachs. Something in Lyons's mind said that nobody could fake that groan. Whatever it was, it wasn't a trick.

Ears straining in the darkness, they listened for any other sound—voices, somebody moving to help the stricken man, a safety going off—anything.

There was nothing to hear.

Acting on intuition rather than reason, Lyons switched on the flashlight again. He shone it on the four bodies ahead of them. From beneath one, a glistening black sheen crawled out and ran along the rock floor.

Dead men don't bleed, any more than they groan.

Lyons stepped over the nearest body and knelt, placing his fingers on the throat of the bleeding man.

There was a pulse, weak and fast. And something else.

The man had no beard, no facial stubble of any kind. In the light, Lyons saw what he already knew—it was another woman, dressed just like the one he had questioned up in the warehouse.

He examined her in the light. She was young, barely twenty, he judged, with heavy black hair that contrasted with her olive face. She was small, almost petite, in her jungle fatigues that looked tragic and ridiculous against the tunnel floor.

As the light fell on her face, the girl shuddered and died.

What a bastard, Lyons thought. Using women—girls, actually—in his fire teams. Then, next to him, Julie stirred and swallowed hard.

Lyons looked at her. Then, with a start, he realized that Kadal was no worse than he was, in this respect, anyway. At least Kadal probably hadn't been in love with the girl he had sent into battle.

Lyons wondered if he and Kadal were just two sides of the same coin.

The Ironman shrugged and got to his feet. A cold certainty had fallen over him. It answered some of his doubts and told him that the big question still lay before him, up ahead around the corner.

Kadal was there, all right. Waiting for him.

The skeleton from his dream was there, too. His bony hand was still on the card, getting ready to turn it over. They were tied at nineteen apiece; an ace or deuce meant the skeleton would win.

To hell with it. Go for it, Lyons thought.

He turned and strode purposefully down the tunnel, away from a startled Julie, heading for the bend, looking for the last card.

"Kadal!" His voice rang in the tunnel.

"I'm here!"

"You're dead, asshole!"

A peal of laughter greeted his challenge. It reminded Lyons of the laughter from the skeleton in his dream. He started running, and charged around the bend in the tunnel.

Beyond the bend, the tunnel widened into something resembling a small room. It wasn't as dark as the tunnel Lyons had come out of. A shaft of weak light slanted in from a slit some six inches wide in the rock ceiling.

Kadal leaped for Lyons, a submachine gun in his hands. He held it like a club and swung it full force at the Ironman.

The steel smashed Lyons's hands and the M-16 he held. The gun went spinning from his grip, the shock from the impact traveling up his arms.

With lightning speed, Kadal swung his own clubbed firearm again, smashing it into Lyons's chest. The blow felt as hard or harder than hitting Mike Schleigle, the Rams rookie, what seemed like a century ago, Lyons thought wryly.

Lyons absorbed the impact and wrenched the gun out of the terrorist's grip. He hurled it away, flinging it against the rock wall where it struck with a metallic clank. Then the two men rushed at one another in a bone-jarring crunch.

Twin roars of hatred tore from both throats.

Both men were incredibly strong.

Both were skilled fighters.

For what seemed an eternity, the two men struggled, each alternately trying to use his own strength and to make use of the other's force.

Suddenly Kadal slipped one arm free and drove a tightened karate fist up at Lyons's throat. It was a blow intended to kill, crushing the cartilage in the throat, swelling and choking the man on the receiving end to death.

Lyons knew there was only one defense, given their positions.

Take it on the jaw.

As the lightning-fast blow streaked toward his throat, the Ironman turned his head to the side and down, tucking his chin into his shoulder. The fist crashed into his jawbone, fracturing it but saving the precious cartilage beneath. Just as quickly, Lyons returned the blow with a short chop to Kadal's ribs. Then, fighting for consciousness, he hurled the stocky man against the wall of the cave.

A meaty smack rang out as Kadal hit the hard stone.

The terrorist bounced away from the wall, ending up on all fours. He shook his head dazedly as his hand snaked to his belt and pulled out a dagger.

Lyons, too, was dazed. He saw the knife come out and took a step backward, drawing his .45 as he did so.

He aimed it at the terrorist's head.

Perhaps six feet separated them—the world's most dangerous assassin, crouched on all fours, dagger clenched in his fist, and the Ironman, the brash ex-cop with the tired eyes.

Lyons smiled faintly and took the safety off the .45, just as a single, sharp gunshot shattered the stillness of the cave.

Kadal's head exploded in a spray of crimson and gray. His body levitated off all fours into what was almost a standing position, then collapsed in a heap.

Lyons spun.

He saw Julie at the bend in the cave. Her M-16 was at her shoulder. Her face was pale but determined. And Lyons could only imagine how the recoil must have aggravated the wound under her arm. As Lyons watched, the rifle shifted a few degrees until it was pointed at him.

His gaze met hers.

She lowered the rifle and took two shaky steps over to the rock wall. Slowly, painfully, she lowered herself into a sitting position on the rock floor.

For a moment all was silent in the cave, except for Julie's labored breathing. Then she looked up at him, grimacing, her eyes dark and cloudy. "I...love you."

"And I, you." His voice was husky.

"Can...we...get out of here?"

Lyons looked at the source of the light. It was too high and too small for anything bigger than a rabbit to get through.

"I don't know," he said simply. "I don't think so. Does it matter?"

Julie shook her head with some effort. "No. Not really, I guess."

"Not to me, either."

He thought of the dream, and before he spoke again, he managed a smile.

He walked over and sat next to her his back against the wall of the cave. Slowly he reached out and took her hand, lacing her fingers with his.

EPILOGUE

The Tri-Lateral Compact never came to pass.

In the wrap-up that followed the mission, Brognola pieced things together. By his reckoning, it happened about the same time that Lyons and FBI Agent Julie Harris were facing Kadal in the tunnel beneath the ruins.

The "it" that managed to stop the signing—where Kadal had failed in his efforts to do so—occurred in Beirut. A bomb went off in the personal car of a Muslim leader, Aknat Muham. He was killed instantly, along with two of his aides.

Muham, in Brognola's assessment, was a wise and compassionate leader of the Muslims. He had been in the forefront of the negotiations on the Tri-Lateral Compact. It had been he who was largely responsible for reaching the uneasy accord among all the Muslim factions, to even get the TLC as close as it was.

Brognola shook his head as he reviewed the facts.

At the same time his Able Team had been facing off Kadal in the underground tunnel, Muham—who kept irregular hours—had called for a car from the embassy.

None ever arrived. Whether this was deliberate or coincidence was never established.

Finally Muham had decided to take his own. He and the others had been blown to pieces the moment the starter turned over.

With his death, the Tri-Lateral Compact also died.

Blancanales and Gadgets made it out.

They had just checked the tunnel and were sprinting back to warn Lyons and Julie that if they hauled ass they could probably make it.

By the same kind of coincidence that in one sense caused the death of the Muslim leader Aknat Muham, Blancanales and Gadgets had been saved as they raced back down the tunnel.

Specifically the Politician, jungle warfare veteran that he was, had stepped on a chunk of rock about the size and shape of a baseball as he ran. The rock had gone out from under him, and he had fallen heavily. Gadgets stopped to help him, and was just pulling his comrade to his feet when the shaft ahead of them collapsed.

But for the rock, they would have been under the cave-in.

Lyons and Julie were rescued the next day.

Blancanales and Gadgets had lost no time in getting out of the ruins and then returning with a party to dig the whole area inside out, if necessary.

It hadn't been. By the time they got out, Julie had blood poisoning from the wound in her side. Lyons's jaw was swollen nearly shut—X rays showed it was broken in four places from the blow that Kadal had delivered.

None of them would forget Lyons's report as they were finally pulled out of the tunnel. As Julie, by then delirious, was air-lifted away from the ruins, bound for a hospital, Gadgets had signaled Lyons to come to the radio-telephone.

Brognola was on the line.

"Stony Man here."

"Lyons here. What's up?"

"You have a report?"

"Yeah."

"What is it?"

"We won."

Brognola had hesitated a minute. Lyons sounded strange, even for Lyons, and it occurred to the Chief of Ops that maybe the Ironman had at last flipped out.

"What do you mean?"

"Kadal's dead. We aren't. Doesn't that mean we won?"

"Are you sure?"

"I'm sure it's Kadal, and I'm sure he's dead. I'm pretty sure we aren't, but a doctor could tell you better."

"How'd it go?"

Lyons eyes were bleak as he replied. "Piece of cake."

Brognola considered this. He thought about saying a dozen things, but this was all he needed for now.

"Very well," he said crisply. "Well done. Stony Man out."

Harper never surfaced.

Brognola also spent some time on that question. One theory was that Harper had tried to take on Kadal and had lost, and that the terrorist had disposed of the body in a way that it hadn't been found.

Brognola didn't buy that. He had to admit it would be like Harper to try to take Kadal himself, but it would not be like Kadal to try to conceal the body. Ultimately he recommended the CIA regard Harper as "missing, presumed dead."

And that's what they did.

TWO WEEKS LATER, Julie received her final clean bill of health, and was released from the follow-up care that had been prescribed after her release from the hospital six days before.

On the way to the airport—Julie and Lyons were going out to California for some well-deserved R and R—Lyons had directed the cab to stop by Chuck Curtis's office at the Homicide Bureau.

The big detective wasn't in.

It didn't matter. Drawing on his cop background, Lyons had weaseled the appropriate stamp out of the secretary for Team Twelve of the Homicide Squad.

She handed it to him. He hit it on the ink pad and tried it on a scrap of paper.

It was just what they had discussed.

The Ironman nodded, then mooched a blank sheet of paper from her. He scrawled a brief note.

"Curtis—thanks for the help on that hooker homicide in the Towers. Lyons."

He then took the stamp and hit it good and hard a couple of times on the paper, once above and once below his note.

"Case closed/Suspect Deceased."

He taped the note to Curtis's office door, thanked the secretary and walked out to rejoin the woman he loved.

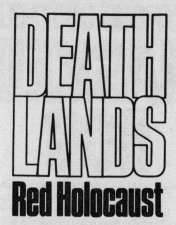

TAKE 'EM FREE
4 action-packed novels plus a mystery bonus

NO RISK
NO OBLIGATION TO BUY

TAKE 'EM NOW

FOLDING SUNGLASSES
FROM GOLD EAGLE

Mean up your act with these tough, street-smart shades. Practical, too, because they fold 3 times into a handy, zip-up polyurethane pouch that fits neatly into your pocket. Rugged metal frame. Scratch-resistant acrylic lenses. Best of all, they can be yours for only $6.99. **MAIL ORDER TODAY.**

Send your name, address, and zip code, along with a check or money order for just $6.99 + .75¢ for postage and handling (for a total of $7.74) payable to Gold Eagle Reader Service, a division of Worldwide Library. New York and Arizona residents please add applicable sales tax.

Remove from pouch...

unfold once...

unfold twice...

and they're ready to wear.

Gold Eagle Reader Service
901 Fuhrmann Blvd.
P.O. Box 1325
Buffalo, N.Y. 14240-1325

Offer not available in Canada.

GES1–RRR